"We're almost out of time, Mercedes. It's been a pleasure, and I suppose we'll agree to disagree."

"I don't think we disagree on everything," she said smoothly. Her voice was polite, almost perfunctory, but Sam knew. There wasn't even an invitation in the words, and certainly not in her eyes. But he knew.

She turned to camera two, seducing the audience just as effectively as she had seduced him.

He knew he was smiling a little too confidently, a little too male, a little too sexually charged, but he couldn't help it.

Something had started the first time Mercedes had been on his television talk show. A flash of lightning, a magnetic pull. And for twelve months it had stayed buried. But no more.

Tonight they were going to finish it.

D0709065

Blaze™

Dear Reader,

I hope you enjoy the final installment of THE RED CHOO DIARIES. It's always bittersweet coming to the end of a miniseries, because a writer develops such a strong relationship with the characters. And if you fall in love with them, you hate to say goodbye. I know I have a soft spot for the Brooks family, which is loosely based on my own sibling relationship and watching the interaction between my kids, too.

So, on to the last book. Mercedes and Sam. It's always fun to watch two people on opposite sides of the fence realize they're meant for each other. It makes for a tough courtship, but you know that if these two have fallen in love, then it's gonna last forever. I hadn't intended Sam to be the hero for Mercedes. He was one of those characters who just walked on, and I saw the sparks between him and Mercedes, and wow! I was suckered right in, and I have to admit that I truly enjoyed writing their story. I don't think I've ever written two characters who had more fun together.

I want to hear from my readers, so please write. My address is Kathleen O'Reilly, P.O. Box 312, Nyack, NY 10960, or kathleenoreilly@earthlink.net. I've received some great letters from readers and I keep them in a special file because when it's raining, or cold, or life gets that little bit harder, I read them again and again. A letter can really touch an author's heart. For the latest news on my next Harlequin Blaze projects, please check at www.kathleenoreilly.com.

As always,

Kathleen O'Reilly

BEYOND SEDUCTION
Kathleen O'Reilly

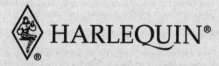

HARLEQUIN®

TORONTO • NEW YORK • LONDON
AMSTERDAM • PARIS • SYDNEY • HAMBURG
STOCKHOLM • ATHENS • TOKYO • MILAN • MADRID
PRAGUE • WARSAW • BUDAPEST • AUCKLAND

ISBN-13: 978-0-373-79325-9
ISBN-10:   0-373-79325-1

BEYOND SEDUCTION

This edition published by arrangement with Harlequin Books S.A.

® and TM are trademarks of the publisher. Trademarks indicated with ® are registered in the United States Patent and Trademark Office, the Canadian Trade Marks Office and in other countries.

www.eHarlequin.com

Printed in U.S.A.

ABOUT THE AUTHOR

Kathleen O'Reilly is the award-winning author of several romance novels, pursuing her lifelong goal of sleeping late, creating a panty-hose-free work environment and entertaining readers all over the world. She lives in New York with her husband, two children and one rabbit. She loves to hear from her readers at either www.kathleenoreilly.com or by mail at P.O. Box 312, Nyack, NY 10960.

Books by Kathleen O'Reilly

HARLEQUIN BLAZE
297—BEYOND BREATHLESS*
309—BEYOND DARING*

HARLEQUIN TEMPTATION
967—PILLOW TALK
971—IT SHOULD HAPPEN TO YOU
975—BREAKFAST AT BETHANY'S
979—THE LONGEST NIGHT

*The Red Choo Diaries

Don't miss any of our special offers. Write to us at the following address for information on our newest releases.

Harlequin Reader Service
U.S.: 3010 Walden Ave., P.O. Box 1325, Buffalo, NY 14269
Canadian: P.O. Box 609, Fort Erie, Ont. L2A 5X3

To Dee, as always, thanks.

1

"Okay, Sam, that's a wrap."

The hot television lights were powered off, and Sam Porter pulled back from the small desk on the sound stage. He took a last drink of his water, and wanted nothing more than to be home in bed, preferably alone, nursing a cold beer, and watching the tape of today's show.

Four a.m. was too early for any human being of sound mind to be up, but he'd sacrificed in order to prep for this interview, which had been a slam-dunk. The Connecticut Senator was political roadkill, although now Sam felt like death warmed over and the night was still young.

The crew began arranging the studio for the next broadcast, cameras being rolled away to the side of the set as the mechanized take-down duties were performed.

He nodded in the general direction of his floor director. "Thanks, Kristin. See you tomorrow."

Kristin winked at him, putting aside her clipboard and headset. "Maybe you'll see me. I've got a hot date— think I'm going to elope."

He rubbed at his face with his palms. "Just as long as you're back in the morning. Don't make me break in another one of you."

"Sure, boss," she answered.

The crew started to take off. Goodbyes were always the shortest when the weekend was lurking nearby. Today was only Wednesday, but his staff were forward thinkers and Friday couldn't come soon enough.

"Sam, wait a minute, will ya?" The voice of his producer boomed over the studio speakers, and Sam scowled in the general direction of the production booth. He wanted to get home, and Charles Whistleborne Kravatz III could be excruciatingly long-winded when he put his mind to it.

Charlie ambled into the studio, squawking into his cell. Impatiently, Sam tapped his foot until Charlie noticed, gave Sam an apologetic smile, and then kept talking for another ten minutes. Sam was just turning to leave when Charlie finally hung up.

"We've got a problem. The city manager pulled out and we've got to find another guest for Thursday's show."

"You're kidding?"

"Sorry, Sam. Your fan base isn't huge out there."

"Yeah, well, someday. So what are we going to do? Know any Northern California radicals to put on?"

Charlie scratched his neck, parting the Brooks Brothers shirt buttons around his ever-expanding stomach. "I think we should do something less political. To offset the judicial expert's talk about the nominee for the Supreme court. Big yawner. Give it some balance."

"Like what?"

"I don't know. Human interest. Fluff."

"I don't like fluff," warned Sam.

"No lectures, Sam. Hear me out. You're doing two solid days of hard, depressing crap. We need something more upbeat. Happier. Maybe not birdies and rainbows, but something to put people in a good mood."

At the moment, Sam was several emotions removed from a good mood. "I don't know, Charlie. Let me think. I'm tired and I need sleep."

Charlie nodded. "Do that. And let me know." He turned around to leave, and then turned back. "Hey, I got a call about you while the show was taping."

"Not another death threat, I hope?"

"Hehe, no. One of your fans. Chairman of your favorite New Jersey political party. He tried to play coy, but I pegged him. They want you to be their drop-in candidate for the House Seat in the Fifteenth District, after Detweiler pulled out. Four months before the election? Who does that?"

Sam started to laugh. "Me? A candidate? You're kidding."

"Nope."

Eventually Sam realized that Charlie was serious, mainly because Charlie was always serious.

Politics. His smile faded. "Really?"

"Yeah. Since we're right up against the election, it's got to be a write-in candidate, and the party knows you've got the name recognition to pull it off. They know they can trust you, your platforms are right. It's not that big of a leap, Sam."

"You're kidding," repeated Sam, still slightly in shock. It was flattering, it was intriguing, and most of all, it was something that he'd never thought about before. "I'm in television. I talk about politics. I don't do politics," he said, weighing the arguments out loud.

"I take it that's a 'no' then. I'll send your regrets."

Sam almost corrected that, but something held him back. "Yeah, just tell them no," he said, finality in his voice.

"Glad to hear it 'cause we'd have to kill the show, and I for one would not be happy. Hell, I'd have to find a new show. And I don't even wanna think about the network. You're a cash cow, and cash cows are hard to come by these days."

"I didn't think about losing the show," Sam murmured, wrapping his mind around the possibility of a new direction in his daily routine.

"You're thinking about losing the show, Sam?" asked Charlie, his faded blue eyes still sharp as they'd always been.

"How long do I have?"

"You gotta decide fast. Ten days is all you've got."

Politics. It was something he talked about, studied, read about on a daily basis, but he'd never considered himself a politician. He was a journalist. But wouldn't it be nice to be able to work for the country instead of bashing do-nothing politicos on a nightly basis? His practical side laughed at the idea, his sentimental side was flush with new ideas.

"I should say no," he answered, his practical side winning the argument. Sam had enough to think about right now. Like what to fill in on Thursday's show.

"But that's not a 'no'?"

"It's a not yet," answered Sam. "I'll take the ten days, Charlie. Let me think."

After Charlie left, Sam headed for the dressing room. Finally a chance to lose the suit, and he pulled on his jeans with a contented sigh. He would never be a suit, and although he played a talking-head on TV, and did it well, blue jeans were his natural habitat.

The television studio was a cold, lifeless place with cameras, overhead banks of monitors, and the smell of sanitized air freshener, rather than the smell of hard work.

Sam's dad had been a plumber, who came home smelling of plumber's grease and somebody's clogged drain pipe, and Sam had learned to appreciate the smells that came with an honest day's labor. It was the primary reason his dressing room smelled like pen ink and microwaved chicken rather than the 'clean fresh scent that follows a soft summer's rain.'

His ratty, overstuffed couch was always waiting for him when he wanted to lay down and think, and the sounds of Bob Dylan, Toby Keith, and Springsteen were permanent playlists on his iPod. He needed it to drown out the city noise. At his heart, Sam was a Jersey boy, born and bred, and although Manhattan paid his salary, his home sat on the blue-collar side of the Hudson River.

Sam cast a longing look at the couch, but he had places to go and people to meet. The couch—and much-needed sleep would have to wait.

Two long East-West blocks covered the distance from the studio to the bar on 11th where he was headed. A few fans stopped, waved, but New York wasn't the target market for the Sam Porter show. A conservative talk show host in Manhattan garnered more death threats than autograph requests. Since Sam was a firm believer in the right to bear arms, as well as carry them, he wasn't fazed.

The cool September air blew around and through the concrete jungle, and it was a great night for a walk, the perfect way to wake him up. It might be Wednesday, but New York never knew it. Midtown was bustling, cabs lined up bumper to bumper, the night lights starting to illuminate the sky. Yeah, city life was okay.

He passed by a bookstore on the way, and the photograph in the window caught his attention. Sam stopped.

He knew that face; a face he'd had on his show—once.

Mercedes Brooks.

It'd been over a year ago, and he'd pushed her from his mind, or so he thought, but the photograph stirred up a visceral reaction that surprised him with both its appearance and its intensity.

He studied the picture. She hadn't changed, her long, long dark hair was deeper than the shadows.

Her eyes were just as dark as her hair, and the photographer had caught a wicked gleam in them.

Those eyes had made him wonder.

Did they tease a man first thing in the morning, or were they cloudy with sleep? Did they ever grow blind with passion, reckless and unknowing?

It might only be a photograph, but the camera had captured a part of her, and the gleam stayed there. How far would she go? A teasing Lolita, a brazen Delilah?

He stood and looked for a minute, happy for the anonymity of a busy street where no one cared if a man stood a little too long, or stared a little too hard.

Then, spurred on by an impulse that he didn't want to examine, Sam walked inside, picked up a book off this display, and started to read. He should've known it'd be a mistake, everything about her yelled "mistake" but he wanted to know, and his eyes followed the evocative words, blood-heating words:

He wasn't a man she'd ever see outside the bedroom, because his world wasn't hers, and she couldn't adapt to his, so they met in private, in the dark, and for a few hours, they would pretend.

She loved lying next to him, his body so much stronger and bigger than hers. Sometimes she would trail her fingers over his arms, following the ridges and dips, the curling hairs tickling the pads of her fingers. He had lovely arms that sheltered her, and kept her warm when the world was cold, cherished her when she felt unloved.

His body was built to pleasure her with his big, hard, workman's hands, among other parts. She loved when he rubbed his hands over her, slow at first, almost shy. He wore a ring on his right hand, cold silver that jarred when he drew it over the heated skin of her breasts. He would do that to her, and at first she thought it was an accident, but by the third time, she grew to love that ring, and the simple wanton pleasure of cold silver against a naked breast. Her breasts weren't the only place he teased. He liked to delve between her thighs, the ring pressing against hot, swollen flesh. A single touch that would pull her out of her skin, but never fast. Always slow, excruciatingly slow…

"Sam Porter?"

The voice jerked him out of that dark, blissful place that he'd just visited with his vivid imagination. He glanced down. At his body.

Quickly he covered his fly with the book and turned. An older woman stood there, her eyes as curious as a kid. She was bundled up in a wool cardigan and carried a stack of books in her hands. "You're reading that?" she asked, the bright eyes dipping to the lurid cover.

Instantly Sam put on his fan-face. "Oh, no. Just keeping up with the state of the world."

She clucked her tongue, the faded red hair shaking in disapproval. He saw that look a lot. "Sad what's happening. Sometimes I think I'm getting too old, that I don't understand the young. Sex, sex, sex. Seems like we get bombarded with it everywhere. Books, television, health insurance. Can you believe it, they're using sex to sell health insurance? You should put that on your show."

Carefully, unobtrusively, Sam replaced Mercedes's sex book, then gave the woman an empathetic nod. "I think you're right. I'll talk to the producer."

The woman stared at the dark, gauzy cover displaying a man and a woman locked in a shameful, wicked, indecent embrace that looked…

Sam looked harder.

…really inviting.

Time to cut to a commercial. "Listen, I need to run. There's never enough time, is there?"

The woman held out her hand, and Sam took it in his two. He'd learned many years ago that women really liked that move, no matter the age.

"Watch us next week. We'll be heading out to San Francisco on Thursday and Friday."

The blue eyes grew wide with shock. "San Francisco? They're very liberal out there, aren't they?"

Sam smiled and gave her his confiding laugh. "New judge on the Ninth Circuit, and there's a legal scholar who's written about the court. I've got some questions. That's the way it starts. I always have questions."

Visibly she relaxed. "That's what I like about you. You won't let anybody get away with anything. I won't miss it. Can I ask you a favor?"

"What can I do for you?"

She held up the stack of books in front of her. Law books. "I got a problem with the social security department. Foolish computer error, that's what it is."

"What what is?"

"They think I'm dead, and I don't know how to prove I'm alive. The state of New York issued a death certificate as a mistake. I was in the hospital four months ago, stupid heart. I should exercise more, I suppose."

"You need some help?"

"Could you?"

Sam thought for a minute. "I'll need your ID. Just to make sure you're not pulling one over on me."

She laughed, and then handed over a well-worn card. "Here you go," she answered.

Sam pulled out his cell, and punched in a few numbers. "I know just the guy.

"Dan. It's Sam. Need a favor—"

"You're not going to put us on the show, are you?"

"No, no, you're in the clear—this time. I have a citizen in need."

"It's after five, Sam. Can it wait?"

"Come on, Dan, I'll owe you one, and best of all, it's easy."

"Will we get a kudos on the air?"

"For you, I'll do a special segment."

"Okay, what's up?"

"I have a lady here, living, breathing, and talking to me, that the social security department thinks is dead. Can we correct the state records, and mail one of your official letters to those nasty bureaucrats in Washington that wouldn't know a heart if it was, well, a living heart?"

"Name of the un-dead?"

"Geraldine Brady," answered Sam, and then reeled off the rest of Geraldine's pertinent info while she beamed as any non-dead citizen would. "Got all that?"

"Yeah. Blockheads, all of 'em. I'll fix it."

"You're a prince among men, Dan."

"Save it for your fans, Sam."

He just laughed and hung up. "I think it's taken care of it, but here's one of my cards, and let me know if you don't get a letter in a couple of weeks."

Geraldine put down her books and gave him a hug. Right in the middle of the bookstore. Sam smiled politely, because he wasn't exactly comfortable with the touchy-feely aspects of his job, especially not under the wicked, gleaming eyes in the photograph of Mercedes. Sam ran a finger under the collar of his leather bomber jacket, feeling the sweat that had collected there. Somehow, some way, he was absolutely sure Mercedes Brooks was laughing at him. He swore under his breath, and shook his head, clearing the ghosts, clearing the image of her.

O'Kelley's was a much-needed reprieve from the bookstore. The place was casual, dark, and ear-poppingly loud. He scanned the room for the guys, spotting them at a table against the black-paneled wall, underneath the Harp beer sign. Bobby was a journalist who he'd bonded with when he was a political reporter for WNBC. Across from him was the reason for the dinner—Tony Rapanelli. Seven years ago, after a particularly rowdy New Year's Eve party, Tony had mistaken Bobby for a mugger and tackled him in the middle of 8th Avenue. It was the start of a beautiful friendship.

Things had been quiet for awhile, but now Tony was going through the last throes of a painful divorce, and it was sucking the life out of him slowly and surely. For the past few months, Sam and Bobby had been working with Tony, trying to cheer him up, trying to let him see life after a break-up. Tony—who had been married for seventeen years, with two kids, two dogs, and one house on Long Island—hadn't even cracked a smile.

However, they were determined to keep trying.

Sam plastered a grin on his face. "Hey! Didn't mean to keep you all waiting."

Bobby stood and they knocked fists, an odd mix of formality and urban America. Although he always wore a jacket, Bobby was half Puerto Rican, half Italian and still carried around some of the ways of the street. "My man, how's things?"

"Eh," Sam answered, ordering a Diet Coke from the waitress.

He settled into a chair and grabbed the bowl of pretzels, the best he was going to manage for dinner.

Tony raised his glass. "To women."

At that, Sam raised a brow. This was new. Maybe they were lucky and Tony had gotten laid. In Sam's experience, sex always put a rosy spin on life.

"Today is Tony's anniversary," muttered Bobby, before Sam could get too carried away with excitement.

"Listen, Tone, the wife has a friend. Now, she's not a stunner, but she's nice—"

The table broke out in groans. "And she got a boob job last year," he finished.

"Age?" asked Tony.

"Thirty-two."

"What's wrong with her?" he asked.

"Now, wait a minute," Sam interrupted. "Tony, you're thirty-seven. Absolutely nothing is wrong with you, and there's no reason to assume that there's a problem." Sam believed in fighting injustices wherever they occurred, even in his friends.

"Point taken," admitted Tony, and then turned back to Bobby. "So what's wrong with her?"

"Were you listening?" said Sam. "There doesn't have to be anything wrong with her. Right, Bob?"

Bob got all shifty-eyed and Sam groaned. "Look, she's got this voice. Kinda Brooklyn."

"No, absolutely not," said Tony, using two syllables at the end, just like any good Long Islander would do.

"Jeez, how do you plan on meeting any women if no one is good enough?"

Bobby laughed at Sam. "Spoken like the eternally single man that you are."

"I was married. Once," said Sam.

Bobby rolled his eyes. "Anything before twenty-six is too young to count."

Bobby was right about that. The marriage had been too short, too casual to count, and Sam had stayed far away since then. Maturity and wisdom would do that to a man. But today, he found himself wishing there was someone to go home to. Not because he wanted a home-cooked meal, oh, no. His reasons were more basic. Sam was still carrying around an extra seven inches of pain and misery from a little too much "cold silver against a naked breast," and it would be nice to have someone to take the edge off.

Like Mercedes Brooks, for example.

Sam closed his eyes and groaned, low and painful, and a mere two decibels louder than he intended.

Tony looked at him sideways. "What's wrong?"

Both his friends were staring, because Sam didn't have problems. He didn't groan. He didn't complain. And usually he didn't suffer from slip of the tongue disease. Lack of sleep, lack of sex seemed to be taking its toll. Damn. Sam shook it off. "It's the show. We got stuck without a second guest for Thursday night. A city manager broke his leg, and now I'm guestless, except for the judge."

"What does Charlie say?"

"He wants to do something lighter."

"What do you want?"

It was a loaded question because up until that moment, Sam would have answered differently, but his whole body was tense and taut, and the more he considered it, the more he thought that maybe Charlie was right. They did need something lighter. More provocative. "Sex."

Bobby howled. "Hard up?"

"I meant for the show."

"Then book a sex therapist."

"No." His mind was racing along various roadtracks, but he kept coming back to the same endpoint.

"A hooker? You know, they're trying to unionize in Canada. That could be both sexual and political."

You know, Bobby had a point, but not now. And not

in San Francisco. Sam was busily pondering other plans for San Francisco. "No."

"Sam, you're boring."

"I'm not boring," he protested.

"So find somebody."

He knew somebody. She'd be the perfect somebody. They could discuss the white-noise of sex in America. She could blissfully talk about sex—meaningless, passionate sex between two consenting adults, locked in a tangle of bare flesh, while he drove inside her, tasting the curve of a firm naked breast...

Damn.

Sam really needed to get laid. It'd been over three months since he'd broken up with Shelia. She'd been nice enough, but she wasn't The One. She wasn't even The Maybe One.

"Book somebody, Sam," said Tony with an almost-smile.

"Great looking," added Bobby. "It's about time that your guests weren't old, fat and bald."

"Can you guys give me a break? Enough about my show, let's talk about something else. Like Tony. The purpose of this dinner. Remember?"

Bobby nodded. "You got to get back on the horse, Tone. Sam'll find some club, you'll meet women, see them all nicely dressed, or undressed, and remind you of what you are."

"What's that?" asked Tony.

Bobby smiled, wide and slow. "You're the rarest of the rare. A precious quantity to be savored and sipped, and tupped as often as you like. You're a single, heterosexual man in New York."

He might as well have thrown his friend in front of a bus, for all the good it did. Tony attempted a weak smile. "I don't know that I can do this."

Tony was going to need all the reassurance he could get. "Don't worry about it," Sam said. "I'll call Franco. He knows the good places." Sam made a note to himself to call Franco, and stuck around for another couple of rounds. But tonight, it wasn't the taste of alcohol that put him on fire. It was one Mercedes Brooks.

On the way home, he stopped by the bookstore in Paramus and picked up a copy of her book, buying it quickly before anyone noticed.

When he got to his house in north Jersey, he settled down to read, and got halfway through the first chapter when he made up his mind. Mercedes Brooks was going on his show. Charlie was right. What would be so wrong with a little talk about sex?

He laughed at himself. Yeah. Since when did he agree with his producer? He looked down at the book, flipped to the cover, watching the faint images come to life in his mind. It wasn't politics he was thinking of now, far from it. She'd stayed there in his head for nearly a year. Maybe it was time to see Mercedes Brooks again.

In the flesh.

2

THE LITERATURE PANEL AT the Algonquin Hotel had been the idea of Portia McLarin, Mercedes's agent. At first, Mercedes had thought it'd be a blast. After all, the Algonquin was a New York landmark for the literati. When Mercedes had stepped through the dark oak entrance, she knew she had made it to the big leagues. At one time, the hotel's Round Table hosted the likes of Dorothy Parker, Edna Ferber and Robert Benchley. And tonight—the one, the only—Mercedes Brooks.

Yeah, right.

There were two other authors besides Mercedes. Linda who wrote fiction, and Cecily the poet. Linda was snazzily attired in a nipped-waist blazer that was probably Marc Jacobs. She'd paired it with jeans and a tie, although the shoes were a little too penny-loafer for Mercedes's taste. All things considered, the outfit was wonderfully chic.

However, the positive aura was spoiled when Linda proudly announced that she had received an MFA from Columbia and wrote "lit-ra-chur." Mercedes slunk an inch lower in the leather-backed chair.

The second girl was Cecily, a Bohemian-vegan type with frizzy brown hair, and wire-rim spectacles, and absolutely no sense of fashion or style. Cecily wrote "abstract poetry" and lived in a warehouse in Brooklyn, no surprise there.

They were only twenty minutes into the discussion, and the bright lights were already starting to make Mercedes sweat, as was the moderator, a stuff-shirted academic. As someone who wrote about sex, and had just published a book of erotic fiction, Mercedes really didn't have the time nor the inclination to deal with someone who desperately needed to get their rocks off, assuming he had any.

"Miss Brooks, can you tell us why you feel the urge to write fiction designed to titillate?" The man's voice sliced down her spine like broken glass, but Mercedes was determined to stand up for the constitution, especially that pesky first amendment.

"Why does any writer need to write?" she asked, dodging the titillate word deftly. "It's part of documenting the human condition."

"But don't you feel your—work," he said, with a dismissive sniff, "reduces the human condition to a training manual on copulation?"

"No, I believe some other literary author won the award for bad sex writing. Not me. I believe my fans are more discerning than that."

He stroked his goatee, quirking one brow. "And what about probing the deep, dark places where man is afraid to tread? Isn't writing about sex selling out?"

"Now, this is only the opinion of one poor, lowly author, but the whole point of writing erotica is to write about those deep, dark places where man is afraid to tread." She turned to Linda, who was the panelist next to her and smiled politely. "What is your book about?"

Linda sat up straight and cleared her throat. "*My* book is a soul-stirring exploration of a mother's love for her children, who murders them in the end, as a tribute to the transcendental nature of life."

The moderator sighed, a goofy fan-girl sigh that pushed Mercedes over the edge. When had a weight the size of the Titanic fallen on the scales of justice? It truly wasn't fair. "And you sniff at my book?"

"I do not sniff at art," the moderator snapped.

"I bet you never break wind, either," Mercedes muttered under her breath.

"I beg your pardon?" asked Cecily.

Mercedes checked her watch. "This has been lovely, but I gotta go. Autographing at Rockefeller Center."

"Rockefeller Center?" asked Linda, her voice embracing the words in a sad lover's caress. Dream on, sister.

"Of course. It's a rite of passage for every author, don't you think?"

Linda nodded, her eyes dreaming of booksignings she would never have, and Mercedes gave her an encouraging pat on the back. "Someday," she said, a hint of encouragement in her voice.

She tried not to strut as she walked off the dais, but okay, maybe there was a kick in her heels. What was success if not to be enjoyed? And after all, somebody needed to right those scales of justice. Mercedes thought she was just the one.

Sadly, her moment of fighting for truth, justice, and the American right to read about sex was fleeting. There wasn't a booksigning in Rockefeller Center; Mercedes had made that one up, being nothing if not creative.

ACROSS TOWN ON THE LOWER EAST SIDE, Mercedes was back in her apartment, which wasn't exactly an apartment, more like a closet with living accessories. The tiny studio had a couch that folded into a bed—when she took the trouble to pull it out. Other amenities included a sink, a one-burner stove, and a half-height refrigerator. At least the bathroom had a tub, her one necessity in life.

She punched the answering machine button and got a message from Andreas.

"Hey, Mercedes, listen, something's come up tonight, so I won't be by. We'll talk later. You're the best."

She hit the erase button with a little more force than necessary, mainly because of the music playing in the background. Okay, he wasn't the world's best boyfriend. Actually she didn't even call him her boyfriend because that would imply some level of emotional foreplay in their relationship, and there was none.

Andreas was like so many guys in the world, not really interested in anything but a good time. Mercedes didn't let it bother her. She wrote erotic fiction, after all, and could chalk the whole relationship up to research and not lose a bit of sleep. Of course, that would imply she didn't lose sleep, which she did. More than she would admit to anybody.

A single woman today was supposed to be hard and emotionless when it came to love and sex, and Mercedes wanted that. When you felt nothing, you didn't hurt, you didn't bleed. After almost ten years of rejections from publishers, it was helpful to grow a thick hide and let the slings and arrows of the world bounce off of you. But sometimes an arrow got through the castle walls, and that's when it was time for a bath—with lavender-scented bubbles to ease the pain away.

Mercedes drew the hot water, pipes clanking as always, and poured in the magic liquid. Quickly she shed her clothes and slipped into the one place where she could hide from the rest of the world. She leaned her head back against the ancient cast-iron tub and closed her eyes. Her dreams weren't easy ones. She wanted to hit the *New York Times* list, somehow, someway, somewhere.

She supposed her life would be less stressful if she wasn't so ambitious but her mother had always encouraged big dreams. Mercedes had always wanted to be a writer, to explore the depths of humanity. The good, the evil, and the sexual. When she started the sex blog, the Red Choo Diaries, it'd been a lark. A way to make a name for herself without having the publishing credits that were required, and make a name she did. The blog had gotten her an agent and a two-book deal. And as a bonus, her brothers had found true love because of the blog. Everyone was happily involved except for her.

The water enveloped her, and she tucked a warm washcloth over her eyes, breathing in the gentle scent. Eventually her body was in another place, a place where her stories lived. That dark, mysterious world were lovers had no faces, and fantasy sex would always be better than reality sex.

Her fingers began to explore the map of her body she had memorized early on. Hiding beneath the bubbles, she could soothe the place between her thighs. While she pleasured herself, she didn't think of Andreas, or Nick, or Alex or any of the lovers she'd had.

Her lover didn't have a name, only the hard hands that she wrote about in her book, the long body she yearned to explore, and the intense eyes that made her want. They would be hazel eyes, green and brown swirled together like watercolors in the rain. Eyes that flashed gold when impassioned, and calmed to the color of summer leaves when they were at peace.

Her body rose in time with his, and the soothing lavender scent only sharpened the molten throbbing at her center. He moved faster within her, a quicksilver image that was not quite real, yet more than a dream. She wanted to touch him, wanted to kiss his mouth, test the heat of his skin, but he was always just beyond her reach.

Right then the phone rang, and Mercedes almost didn't bother, but an unanswered phone was like an unscratched Super Match For Millions ticket.

"Hello," she answered, trying not to be peeved. The person on the other end didn't need to know they'd interrupted a climax in progress. Although if it was a telemarketing call, her peeve was going to be out in full force.

"Mercedes Brooks?" asked a voice. A resonant, confident, sexy voice.

"Yes?"

"Sam Porter."

Sam! Mercedes fumbled to keep the towel and the phone in place. "Hello, Sam," she purred, sounding completely poised. Mercedes could fake it like the rest of them.

"So, has your brother hit anybody else recently?"

Oh. "I was hoping you'd forgotten." It'd been almost a year since her brother, Jeff, had punched Sam out on live TV when she'd been a guest on his show. A few mistaken impressions, a bunch of wrong words. Not a high moment in her life.

"No, the jaw still aches sometimes."

"You'll never let me forget that, will you?"

"Probably not."

"You insulted the woman he loves. What would you have done?"

"The celebrated gossip of tawdry celebrities was the topic of the show. I don't pull my punches."

"Neither does he," Mercedes said proudly. "So why did you call?"

"We're shooting in San Francisco next week, and I was wondering if you'd want to come on the show."

Ca-ching! Mercedes squeezed her fingers on the towel to keep from squealing. Never a smooth move. He wanted her on the show? Not the perfect audience for erotica, but hey, she wasn't going to complain, with her book just hitting the shelves. Mercedes did a short happy dance before regaining her poise. "What day were you thinking?"

"We'd have you on Thursday night. Fly you out there on Thursday, fly back on Friday. The show would pick up the tab."

Such mundane words, in such a lustrous voice. Soft, intimate, infinitely warm. Jeez, he was talking travel arrangements and she was getting seduced. "What do you want to talk about?" she asked, trying to keep all those seduce-me fixations out of her brain.

"It's only a short segment. The meat of the program is going to a judicial scholar who just published a book on the Ninth Circuit's influence on the Supreme Court, so we'd only have about ten minutes. The topic would be how the white noise of sexual messages is negatively affecting the libido."

"I'm assuming that I'm the face of the sexual white noise?" she asked dryly, no longer full of seduce-me fixations.

"Uh, yeah. Not me."

She sighed heavily into the phone, disappointed because, well, she didn't want to analyze why she was disappointed that Sam Porter wasn't murmuring erotic nothings over the phone.

"You'll do it?" he asked.

Like she would say no. "You'll send me the travel arrangements?"

"Charlie's assistant will call you."

"Thank you for thinking of me, Sam."

"It wasn't hard. You're not easy to forget."

Mercedes pumped a fist into the air. "Twelve months is a long time to sit idly by."

"Yeah, congratulations, by the way," he said, easily slipping back to his smooth, melodious television voice. No intimacy, all professional.

"For what?"

"The book."

"You knew?"

"I do read."

"You read it?" she asked, not bothering to hide the surprise. Sam's political leanings didn't lend themselves to erotica. Damn it.

"No, but I have been spotted in bookstores before, Mercedes."

"You don't approve, do you?"

"It's not my place to approve or disapprove. Free country. Free speech. That's what makes America great."

She laughed softly, sensing the truth. "You hate it."

"No. Honestly."

He was a liar. But what was the point in calling him on it? "How are you doing? The show's ratings are through the roof."

"You noticed?"

"I do watch TV."

"My show?"

"Sometimes," she answered, not wanting to tell him that she taped his show and watched it before bed. She liked listening to him at night, and his opinions weren't *that* kooky. At least most of the time. Sometimes, when she was really, really tired, she even agreed with him. But she would never tell him that.

"I need to go. Thanks for doing this."

"Sure." Mercedes hung up the phone, and returned to the bathroom. The water was cool to the touch, so she ran a brand-new tubfull, making it warm and soothing. She touched herself again, her fingers taking up where they had left off, and she returned to the dark, mysterious world where her lovers resided. But this time, her lover had a face and a voice.

Hazel green eyes, firm lips, a nose that looked like it'd been broken once, and silky, tawny brown hair that fell any way but straight.

As she slipped into the last wake of her climax, she thought of Sam and smiled.

BERGEN COUNTY, NEW JERSEY, was as close to nature as a man could be, yet still be less than thirty minutes from

Manhattan. Sam owned three shaded acres of towering Douglas firs, and grass growing as it was meant to be, not trimmed into some geometrical hoodoo. His office was in the back of the house, where he could watch Max, his black lab happily chase squirrels. At the moment, instead of chasing squirrels, Max was happily snoozing, leaving Sam to his own thoughts.

A man with an MA, BA and BBA, shouldn't be thinking of T & A when contemplating his livelihood. He was a professional, a man who'd been yelled at, threatened, and yes, hit once, on national television, and never, ever lost his cool. He could think of a million and one reasons why he shouldn't be asking Mercedes to San Francisco. Number one. He was too old for her. He was thirty-nine, and she was a *young* twenty-something. That age when the world was full of opportunity and birthdays were still celebrated. Sam wasn't old by any means, but he'd seen it, he'd done it, and he'd settled into a comfortable existence that didn't involve night-life and a tingling anticipation of tomorrow. For God's sake, he had a recliner. Twenty-somethings didn't date men with recliners.

And the reasons didn't stop there. She wrote erotic fiction. Not children's books, not historical fiction, not self-help books. Well, if you really wanted to split hairs, you could consider erotic fiction self-help, but Sam wasn't a hair-splitter. He believed in facts. Honor, responsibility, not just s-e-x, the consummation of a man and woman, bodies entwined together, lost in the mindless passion of the moment, possibly in a recliner.

Why now? Was he approaching a midlife crisis before he hit forty? He'd always been mature for his age, maybe this was just early onset midlife crisis. And did he want to have sex with Mercedes merely to satisfy some arbitrary whim to have a young, hot babe on his arm. God, he didn't even like the word "babe"—or the men who said it.

He swore and Max, his black Lab, lifted his head from the rug and stared.

"What are you staring at?" snapped Sam.

Max turned his head and whined.

"I know it's not smart, Max. But let me work through this. I'll have one night, maybe two. Just to get it out of my system. Then I'll come back, trade in the Lexus on a bright red Ferrari. Like I'm supposed to."

Max cocked his head.

"You can ride in the front seat, the wind blowing through your ears. It'll be just like in the movies. A man and his dog. You got to back me up on this. Tell me I can be strong."

Max barked at him, and Sam smiled. Of course, then he picked up Mercedes's book and started to read again.

Thursday night couldn't come soon enough.

THEY'D PUT HER IN FIRST CLASS. *First class.* If Sam Porter wanted to impress her, he'd certainly started out right. Not that she could be bought, but she could certainly be pampered. Okay, he was conservative. Okay, he was a few years older (and more experienced). Okay, he was unbendable. Nobody was perfect. And what he lacked in other areas, he made up for in physiology.

The flight attendant approached. She knew Mercedes by name, knew her meal preferences, and Mercedes suspected the flight attendant knew her zodiac sign, too. That was service. Not that she could be bought.

"Something for you to drink," the attendant asked.

Mercedes thought for a minute. Unlimited alcohol. Work. Unlimited alcohol. Work. Eventually her puritan work ethic smacked her party girl self into submission.

"Water, please. I have to work," she said, frowning to express her extreme displeasure with the situation.

The man in the seat next to her ordered a scotch and water. "I don't have to work," he told Mercedes with a grin best termed lecherous.

"That's very nice of you. I don't mean to be rude, but I do need to work," she told him, keeping her face airplane-attendant polite.

"You don't mind if I watch, do you? I bet you're really fun to watch. Go ahead, unwind, relax. Make yourself comfortable. When the ladies are hot as you are, I love to watch. *Everything,*" he added, like she really needed that bit of personal info.

A four-hour flight to SFO, and she was stuck next to Mr. McCreepy instead of Dr. McDreamy. Or for instance, Sam?

Mercedes gave the man her cold, formal smile—a smile learned when her mother had tried out for the Broadway version of *My Fair Lady.* Her mother hadn't got the part of Lady Ambassador, but Mercedes had learned how to chill out the world with one look.

McCreepy didn't take the hint. "Are you going to San Francisco for business or pleasure?" he asked, his voice lingering on "pleasure."

"Business," she answered briskly, not quite the truth. There was a good shot of pleasure in the motivational equation for this trip, and she hoped that Sam was equally motivated. There had been sparks when they'd met a year ago. Huge, galaxy-bending sparks, and he'd felt them, too. But Sam was a master of self-control, or he must be to deny the pull of animal magnetism that drew them together. Actually, it wasn't as much animal magnetism as it was his voice, his eyes, those long, capable fingers—okay, maybe it was animal magnetism. Maybe he had endured twelve, long torturous months of monk-like celibacy, because there was only one sultry siren that was woman enough to satisfy his manly urges. And maybe he had come to the realization that a night of passion was their destiny. Sam and Diane. Sam(pson) and Delilah. Sam and Mercedes. Fate. Kismet. Karma. As a card-carrying member of the creative arts, Mercedes believed strongly in the power of all three. Finally he had decided to sample her wares, swim in her unchartered waters, or pluck the nectar from her core. Either way, whether sampling, swimming, or plucking, she was wild about the possibility.

"…and then I was out drinking with this Hollywood movie star…"

Mercedes emerged from her Sam-induced haze and realized McCreepy was talking—strike that—lying to her.

"Were you speaking to me?" she asked, as if there was some possibility that he wasn't.

McCreepy's mouth tightened into a single, hard line. Yeah, well, he'd get over it.

Mercedes's face cracked into a smile and then she pulled out her computer. She had written seventeen pages of her next manuscript, with only two months left to go. And three hundred and thirty-three pages. Softly she hummed "To Dream the Impossible Dream." Not that it was impossible, but late nights and caffeine were definitely on her schedule. Definitely.

The flight attendant returned with her water and McCreepy's drink. "We're going to be stuck on the tarmac for another twenty minutes, are you sure you don't want anything stronger?" the attendant asked.

Mercedes shook her head, noticed McCreepy's wayward gaze, and took out her cell as a further instrument of deterrence. Quickly she dialed her brother.

"Jeff," she said loudly, happily, and hopefully deterrently.

"What are you doing? What do you want?"

Jeff mistrusted his sister more than the normal level of sibling distrust, perhaps due to some past entries about him—anonymously—showing up in her sex blog. However, she had done it all to further the course of true love for Jeff and Sheldon—and perhaps further her own career. A win for all involved, though Jeff didn't see it that way.

"I'm sitting at JFK, waiting for takeoff. A big yawner. Thought I'd kill some time, and you were first on the speed-dial list."

"You're going to be okay on the show?"

"Oh, yeah. I mean, I thought about asking you, but then, what if you hit him again? Then where would I be?"

"It was only one shot, and I didn't even hit him hard."

"Yeah, you say that now that you're safely married. I remember you telling Sheldon how you were ready to kill the guy. Remember that?"

"Maybe I exaggerated."

"You're in P.R. Exaggeration is your life choice. However, I don't think you did that time. What's your better half doing?"

"Sheldon?"

"Well, yes, she is the better half in your matrimonial partnership."

"Love you, too, Mercy."

"What's she doing?"

"I can't tell."

"Of course you can tell, I'm your sister. We must share all. Especially secrets." Sheldon always had the best secrets.

"So you can post it on the Internet? Sorry. Been there, hated that."

"I don't talk about hausfraus in the blog. They're boring unless they're on Wisteria Lane. Not good for getting the eyeballs into my space. What's she doing?"

"Can't say."

"Can to."

"All right. I could, but I won't."

"That's so mean."

"That's me. Your mean, elder brother, Jeff."

"No, that's Andrew. You're nicer, have a better sense of humor, and always gave me cooler birthday presents. Although, if you *don't* tell me, then you're usurping that title."

"Not telling. I'm usurping."

Mercedes slunk further in her seat. "Is it sexual in nature?" Jeff's wife had a certain wild-child reputation before they were married. Sexual in nature would be right up her metaphorical alley.

"No. It's philanthropical."

"Really? Sheldon's doing philanthropy? That's very industrious of her."

"I think so. Are you going to be back by Saturday? Jamie's got some wedding things to do. Sheldon will be mad if you make her go by herself."

Mercedes bit back a groan. "Wedding things? It's the bridesmaid dresses, isn't it? She decided against the silver ones, didn't she?" Jamie was about to marry Mercedes's older brother Andrew, and the whole family was preparing for The Event. Mercedes liked Jamie well enough, but Jamie was cut from a different cloth than Mercedes. Jamie's cloth was more like a scratchy burlap, and Mercedes lived for silk. Still, Jamie made Andrew happy, and Andrew wasn't by nature a happy person, so Mercedes let them be. Except for the dress fittings. Five fittings for five different dresses? That didn't make anybody happy.

"I don't know. I can't follow the whole saga. Talk to Sheldon. Better yet, talk to Jamie."

"She'll make me try on dresses again."

"You like trying on dresses, Mercedes. And shoes. And frou-frou blouses, and—"

"That's enough. And this is not the same."

"It's the same."

"It's a root canal, dressed in virginal white."

"That's no way to talk about the happiest day in your brother's life."

"It's going to be the happiest day in my life at this rate. No more bridesmaid dresses."

"Andrew's trying to talk Jamie into something big and expensive for the wedding."

Now this was interesting. "Our brother. Andrew?

Overly work-focused, and driven by the bottom line, Andrew?"

"The same. He's changed."

"I don't believe it."

"He's talking to a wedding planner."

"Does Jamie know?"

"Of course not. I believe her exact words to Mom were 'a wedding planner is an unnecessary occupation designed to take advantage of women in a fragile psychological state.'"

"So what's he thinking?"

"Doves."

"Chocolate?"

"No, the kind with wings. White, flying creatures."

"No way. Not ever. Not even in like ten million years."

"Oh, yes."

"Jamie will hate it."

"I talked him out of it."

"Sensible."

"But not the orchestra."

"Oh, no…"

"Yup. Can't wait till she finds out. Fireworks, big time. Listen, I have to go—"

"No!" Mercedes pitched her voice low, casting a furtive glance in McCreepy's direction. "We're not finished with our conversation."

"Yes, we are."

"No, we're not. I never get to talk to you, Jeff. And you're my favorite brother."

"Mercedes, hang up now."

"I have to stay on the line until they turn off all cell phones and electronic devices."

"You're not afraid of flying."

"That's not my issue."

"What's wrong?" he asked, and she was pleased to note actual concern in his voice.

"Nothing," she said.

"You're going to have sex with him, aren't you?"

"Who?"

"Don't think I don't know, Mercedes. I know you. I saw the way you were ogling him."

"That was twelve months ago, we were live on camera, and if I ogled, it was only for two minutes. This time, I'm going to promote my career."

"Is that what they call this?"

"Don't be insulting."

"You were the one who brought up your career."

"I'm not going to do *that*."

"Yeah. Right."

"Besides, I have a boyfriend." She raised her voice so that the McCreepy could hear. "I'm very devoted to Andreas."

"Mom said you two broke up. Sheldon thinks you're flying out to San Fran to do Sam on the rebound from Andreas."

"I'm not rebounding."

"We'll talk when you get back. I bet you rebound."

"We will not talk."

"We'll see."

"I'm hanging up now."

"Goodbye."

Click.

Immediately Mercedes dialed her brother again. "You did that on purpose, didn't you?"

"What?"

"Made me mad so that I'd hang up and you'd be free to do whatever you needed to do."

"Yup. Saw right through me. Bye, sis." *Click.*

Mercedes punched speed-dial.

"I'm not talking to you."

"You will talk to me."

"I have to go, Mercedes."

"You can't leave me alone with him!"

"Sam?"

"Not Sam. McCreepy."

"Who?"

Mercedes glanced at her seatmate who was staring at her curiously. She tried the cold look again. He smiled back. Mercedes sighed into the phone. "Go do whatever you need to do, and if I die on this plane, a fireball exploding in the heavens, then you'll live with the crushing guilt weighing down your shoulders for the rest of your life."

"Put it in your next book, Mercy. I'm guilt-free."

"Not if we crash."

"You're not going to crash."

"You don't know."

"Flying is safer than driving."

"I live in New York. I don't drive. Flying is not safer than not driving."

"Okay. Rephrase. Flying is safer than jaywalking on Broadway, and I know you jaywalk on Broadway."

"I can't believe you. I'm going to die, and you don't care."

"Can we not talk about airline crashes? I have to go work up a proposal for an airline, and this is really putting me in the wrong state of mind."

"Go. Go off and do whatever you need to do. Forget about your family, the people who love you and have stood by you all these years. The people who worked hard to get you with the love of your life."

"You trashed her in your blog."

"Because it was the only way to get you two together."

"You're going to keep throwing that in my face until I'm old, aren't you?"

"No. Maybe."

"I have to go, Mercedes. Really this time. I'm sure you're not going to crash, but in case you do, I want you to know that I love you, and you're the best sister I've ever had."

"We're not going to crash," she muttered tightly.

"Well, you might. And if you do, I don't want to live with crushing guilt, so I love you."

"You do not," she said, and then quickly hung up. There. If she was going to die, he was going to have to live with crushing guilt.

She powered off her phone, opened her computer, and prepared to work, picking up at the spot where she'd last written…

There were times when she wanted to go into a bar, find a man, and screw his brains out. Not for the sex, not for the intimacy, but for the shock of adrenalin to her system. The danger, the mystery, the feeling of taking a step off a cliff into the air, not knowing if you'll fly or fall. He was that cliff, that leap of faith, but deep in her heart, she knew she couldn't fly. Was it worth it to begin a love-affair doomed from the start? She opened the curtains on her apartment, letting the warm rays of the sun touch her. She loved the morning, loved the feeling of a new beginning. She looked to the building across from her, and noticed the man. He was there everyday, sitting at his desk, talking on the phone, typing. A boring, nondescript existence.

She smiled to herself, smiled to him, and began the morning ritual. Her fingers worked the buttons on her pajama shirt slowly, parting each one, letting the fabric caress her skin as she peeled the shirt back. From beneath her lashes she peeked across the way, feeling his gaze on her. The sun touched her as a lover would, tracing a path across her belly, her breasts, her shoulders.

Carefully she folded the top, putting it on the back of her couch, before slipping her fingers under the edge of her bottoms and pushing them down to the floor. For a moment she stood, framed in the window, nude, enjoying the warm rays on her skin, enjoying the feel of a man's eyes on her body.

She looked up, and met his gaze, and felt the urgency inside him. It echoed the urgency in her. The need to do more, to drink life in long, dragging gulps.

Normally, this was where she stopped. Her body was one thing, to share her secrets was another. But today she could taste the thrill of adventure on her tongue, in her nerves, pulsing through her blood. Across from her, the man wasn't smiling, merely watching. Waiting.

When she hesitated, he picked up his phone and began to talk, his fingers dancing on the keyboard. Back to his meaningless, nondescript existence. Back to her meaningless, nondescript existence.

It was time, that moment of stepping to the edge of the cliff.

She sank into her chair, the comfortable old chair that kept her from being alone, and parted her thighs. His head turned, his fingers stilled, and even from here she would see how his conversation slowed. She leaned back, arching into the soft cushion. At first, her fingers stroked her breasts, gliding over her nipples, back and forth. Gently, as if she were—

A nervous cough jerked her back to reality. She looked over to see McCreepy ogling the words on her computer. Gah! She slammed the lid shut and stared. "Do you mind?"

"What was that?"

"I'm an author," she stated flatly, her tone missing the usual zest that she put in the words.

"That's going to be in a book?" His eyes widened, in such a hopeful manner, she almost forgave him. Almost.

"Yes."

"What's the title?"

Mercedes debated, her sense of security vying with her sense of marketing and sales. Marketing and sales persevered. "*The Return of the Red Choo Diaries.* It'll be out in the fall of next year."

"I'll buy it."

"Thank you," said Mercedes, putting on the complimentary headphones. She didn't dare open her computer again all the way to San Francisco.

3

THE RITZ-CARLTON SAT HIGH on Nob Hill, the city laid out before it like a serf at the feet of his liege. Sam stood at the window, watching as tiny pinpoints of silver moved through the sky, planes approaching the airport. She was out there. Somewhere.

Sam frowned. He had work to do and he couldn't stand here daydreaming. He, Kristin and Charlie were camped out in his hotel suite, planning for tonight's show, but Sam was having a mighty hard time concentrating.

"What time is the judicial expert scheduled at the studio?" he asked, letting the curtain fall, covering the sky.

"Six," Kristin answered.

"And Ms. Brooks?"

Kristin checked her watch. "Her plane just landed."

"Where'd you book them?"

She looked at him, confused. "The supreme court expert? He lives here."

"Ms. Brooks?"

"At the Lafayette, down by the wharf."

The wharf. That was a long away. A good twenty minutes by cab to the Ritz-Carlton. It wasn't a sterling reflection on his character that he was planning a seduction with all the precision of a military campaign. His viewers would be shocked, hell, even he was shocked. It shouldn't be like this. A man shouldn't feel this internal combustion inside him once he got out of puberty. He was too old and too settled. A thirty-nine-year-old man should be contemplating his sanity, his golf game, and his retirement package.

"The Lafayette?" he asked, forgetting about his retirement, and wondering why Mercedes wasn't staying at the Ritz.

"Yeah. Why?" Kristin asked. "It's four stars, Sam, and I love their desserts. You should try the crème brûlée. Fabulous. She'll love it."

Sam pulled a face, not wanting to hear about four stars and fabulous crème brûlée. "The last time I stayed there, I really hated the room I was in. Heater didn't work, and there was some dark stain on the pillows that I didn't want to know about. It's a dump. We should move her. I don't want to give that place any more business. Exercising my consumer rights, and being a good American."

"The Lafayette? We're talking about the same hotel?"

"It's a dump," he lied.

"Okay, Mr. Good American, her plane's at the airport, driver waiting. Where do you suggest I move her to in the next five minutes?"

Sam pretended to think over this problem. Then he got a look in his eyes that he hoped looked like enlightenment rather than ball-busting lust. "Call downstairs. I bet this place has an extra room available."

Kristin grinned. "I'm at the Lafayette. Can I move, too?"

"Sure," he said, knowing the bean counters would

have a fit, but he could handle them. Sam looked at Charlie. "You're here, right?"

Charlie didn't hesitate. "Of course."

"Good," said Sam, nodding. "So, we're all settled in the lodging department. You have the video of the judge's confirmation hearings?"

"Yeah, we'll cut to that after you finish with the discussion of the affirmative action ruling."

"Charlie, did he weigh in publicly on the age discrimination case against the State of Massachusetts?"

Charlie shook his head once. "I don't know, but I'd be surprised."

"Find out, will you?"

"Sure thing."

"Good, the bit with Mercedes should be easy. We've got what, ten minutes, with one break?"

Kristin nodded, so Sam continued on. "And then there's seven minutes of commentary on alternative energy and nuclear power?"

"I thought that was six."

Sam looked at Charlie. "Six or seven?"

"Seven. Definitely seven."

"Okay, all, I think we're set. Great job as always. Will see you in the studio at five."

They left Sam alone, and he went back to the window, not thinking about judicial confirmations. What started as an ache had changed into something more, and all because of a book. That damned one-dimensional book was a peek inside her mind and her fantasies. She had opened that door, and Sam couldn't bear to close it. It sounded like the first throes of a midlife crisis.

Or at least he hoped it was.

MERCEDES SAT IN THE television studio's waiting room, listening to the quiet tick-tick-tick of the clock on the hospital-white wall. If she were a dedicated writer, she would have remembered to bring her computer with her so she could work while she waited, instead of listening to the constant beat of the chronographic version of Chinese water torture.

Tick-tick-tick.

She wiped her palms on her knees, wishing there was a mirror in the place to check her make-up. This wasn't a room designed for comfort, the sterile interior was designed to maximize nervousness—and it was working. Any second now her make-up was going to smear from her sweating—and that was in spite of the forty degree ambient temperature in the room.

Man, she was a basket case. She should have brought Jeff with her. He could have sat next to her, argued with her, and in general, keep her relaxed. But Mercedes was alone in the panic room. Where was Sam?

And then there was the matter of her wardrobe.

She'd packed three outfits for the show, trying to decide between Donna Karan professional or Fighting Eel sultry. And then she'd thrown in an Ella Moss blouse and skirt because wardrobe choices shouldn't be a life-altering decision, but it felt like one. What if her career tanked because she wore a buttoned-up blazer, rather than opting for a little cleavage?

Back at her apartment, she tried on all three, finally zeroing in on the cleavage. Nothing slutty, of course. She was a professional, but if she was the face of the sexual white noise of her generation, she needed to look the part. But she packed them all. And when she got to the hotel, she'd stuck with her original decision. Cleavage.

Tick-tick-tick.

Where the heck was Sam? The other time she'd been on the show, he'd seen her before the show started. What did it mean if he wasn't going to see her this time? Was that a bad sign? It was probably a bad sign. It'd been twelve months, twelve months was a long time. He probably had a girlfriend now. Hell, what if he had a wife? He hadn't had twelve months of monk-like celibacy, he'd been going at it like bunnies with his new bride!

No. He wasn't married. She was getting spazzed up over nothing. Mercedes took a deep breath. She wasn't going to assume the worst. And who said that if he was married now, it was the worst? She didn't need him. There were lots of single men in the waters of Manhattan. Lots. She was single, attractive, and had a certain *je ne sais quoi* that men seemed to go for. Sam was nothing to her.

Nothing. Nothing. Nothing.

Tick. Tick. Tick.

Oh, God. She was going to scream and she hadn't even pondered the matter of the hotel yet.

Her hotel had been changed to the Ritz-Carlton, so what did that mean? It had to be a good sign, and she had to admit that her room was nice and cheery, and then there was the small fact that it was the Ritz. *The Ritz.*

Where was Sam?

"Ms. Brooks?"

She flew out of her seat, realized it wasn't Sam, and took in more oxygen in her lungs.

"Mercedes Brooks?" he asked, his face creased into a tired smile.

"Yes," she answered, casually sitting back down and crossing one leg over another.

"I'm Jacob. Sam won't be here to talk to you directly, so I wanted to go over the instructions. Have you ever been on television before?"

A confident laugh emerged from her lips. "You didn't see me on the show last year, did you?"

"Sorry, no. I'm local to the San Francisco area, so I don't get to see it much," he said. "Bet you were great."

Mercedes made a circle with her hand. "Thanks."

"So, you write erotic fiction, is that right?"

"Yes, I have a copy of the book if you'd like to read it?"

He looked around and then smiled in a secret manner. "I already have. Very. Very. Hot."

"Really?" she asked. "Wow."

"My girlfriend loved it and she gave it to me."

"Wow," Mercedes repeated, sounding just like a gauche, non-sophisticate, but okay, it was cool.

"Oh, yeah. You're going to have to autograph one later."

"Not a problem. So you have instructions for me?" she asked, because as much as she liked the little ego-bits, she needed to stay focused, sharp, and ready for action.

Jacob took the chair next to her and proceeded to go over the layout, and while he was talking, all she could think was, "Where was Sam?" She needed someone here. A familiar face. A familiar voice. The familiar brown sports jacket that he wore a lot of times on Thursday nights.

National TV. Jeez. What had she been thinking? No, no reason to panic, she'd done this before. With a blood relative sitting next to her.

Jacob droned on, and Mercedes hoped it sunk into

her subconscious because her consciousness had left the building.

"Got all that?" Jacob asked.

"Oh, sure," she said with a wave of her hand. "Walk in the park."

After that, she sat alone in the room. Alone in the room with the damned clock.

Tick. Tick. Tick.

"Mercedes?"

The voice. She knew the voice. Sam. Oh, thank you, thank you, thank you. He was silhouetted in the doorway, his hand holding the doorjamb, as if poised for flight. Her expression was probably goofier than she wanted, but she was so happy to see a familiar face. His face. Okay, there was nothing wrong with goofy.

"Hi, Sam."

"Ready?"

"Sure," she lied. Mainly she needed to find a bathroom, because in a few seconds she might possibly lose her lunch.

"Good. See you in about twenty-five minutes."

"Sounds great," answered Mercedes in a faux-cheerleader voice, even though she had never been a cheerleader, and had never wanted to be a cheerleader. She watched him leave.

Tick. Tick. Tick.

Oh, God.

KRISTIN WAS COUNTING DOWN, Mercedes was seated across from Sam, a mere eighteen inches across from him, and all he could do was study the tiny silver ring on her finger. Why did she have to wear a silver ring?

He swallowed, got a last glimpse at his notes, and prepared for the camera.

"Back in three, two, one."

"And we're live." Camera three picked him up, and Sam blinked before his innate skills kicked in to save him. "Tonight, we have as our guest, Mercedes Brooks, author of *The Red Choo Diaries,* a work of rather steamy fiction. Ms. Brooks, welcome to the show."

"It's good to be back."

"So, I caught a glimpse of your book in the store, read some, and when I was reading, all thoughts worth anything flew out of my head. National debt? Not a problem. Trade deficit? No big whoop. Failure of the educational system? What's that? Within two pages, my brain was pretty well smashed."

Her full lips curved into a warm, welcoming smile. "I think that's the point, Sam. We have so many serious problems in the world now, it's nice to forget sometime. To get so carried away with a moment, that you don't have to worry about the national debt, the trade deficit, failure of the educational system, or even carting clothes to the laundry."

"It was nice to get carried away, certainly. But we're getting messages like yours on a daily, heck, hourly basis. Advertisers are using sex to sell every product from soup to health insurance. Now how is that going to help anything? Sex shouldn't be thought of strictly as entertainment. What happened to the emotion behind the act?"

"Done correctly, it's still there."

He wanted to change topics to something less heated, and something less Johnson-hardening, but sex was the point of this segment. It'd been his idea. Stupid idea.

However, he had to stay on point. Sam swallowed and gathered his thoughts. Quickly he dove right into the mix. "But sex is one of those primitive drives. It's not a corporate brand; it goes much deeper. If everything uses sex to sell, sex to entertain, sex to tease, then it becomes nothing more than a brand." *There, that one was safer.*

"But you're forgetting that we need sex. We need sex to procreate, to reduce stress, to live longer, to keep our heart healthy, to make us happier, more functional people."

"But if we're busily engrossed in all things sex, the function goes out the window."

"Has your function gone out the window, Sam?" she asked, the wicked gleam flickering in her eyes, and Sam's brain function went out the window. Every inch of him was focused on her, the gleam in her eyes. He had to see that gleam when they were making love.

He tried not to smile, but camera 2 might have caught it. "Do you ever feel bombarded by sexual messages, Mercedes?"

"Sometimes."

"But after being filled with all that pressure, doesn't it diminish the desire for sex? Maybe not for men, of course, we're not that analytical when it comes to it, but what about for women?"

"There are ways to relieve that pressure," she reminded him in a schoolteacher's voice.

Sam shifted uncomfortably, because he didn't need a hard-on right at that exact moment. Not now. He glanced up at the clock behind the cameras. Three more minutes. All he had to do was get through three more minutes. Quickly he charged into another question. An even safer question.

"Does it bother you that you write about sex? Does anyone tease you about it being cheap or degrading to women?"

Mercedes flicked back her hair, and he glimpsed anger in her eyes. Anger was much better than that sexy, come-hither gleam. "Sex is empowering to women," she started. "It may take us longer to get where we want to go, but the end result is just as sweet. Why can't women be aroused? Why should we be afraid to admit it?"

"Personally, I don't think you should be afraid to admit it. Do many women feel that same way? Afraid?"

"I know I'm not the only one."

"So, when you write about sexual freedom, from a woman's point of view, you're celebrating the woman's desire and control of sex? Interesting. Do you believe in love, Mercedes?"

"Absolutely."

"How do those two work together? From an empowered, sexually liberated woman's point of view?"

He watched her small, white teeth nip into her lower lip. She was fascinating to watch, thoughts flying across her face, until the dark eyes widened, and the full lips split into a satisfied grin. "We all crave love as much as we crave sex. In some ways, even more. That's deeper, more insidious than sex. People kill for love. Not so much for sex. Sex can be an expression of that love, or it can be a hit of pleasure, but just because you're not in love with someone, doesn't mean that sex is wrong."

"And the dangers of sex?"

"You talk about responsibility all the time on your show. There's nothing wrong with sexual responsibility."

"But when you get carried away? When your brain gets smashed, how do you remember? What if you forget?"

"You can't forget."

"But sometimes you do."

"That's not good, and that's not what I want to represent to my readers. Sex has consequences. Good and bad, and you have to prepare for those consequences. If you're not prepared, you shouldn't have sex."

"But isn't that the silver, uh, brass ring for erotica? Two people so carried away that they forget the stresses and the responsibilities and they act on very deep, primitive impulses, stimulated by the very media messages that you provide."

She laughed. "I just write books."

"So did George Orwell and Sinclair Lewis. They changed the world with their books."

"That's some pretty big company I'm expected to keep."

Out of the corner of his eye, he got the signal from Kristin. Thank God. "We're almost out of time, Mercedes. It's been a pleasure, and I suppose we'll agree to disagree."

"I don't think we disagree on everything," she said smoothly. Her voice was polite, almost perfunctory, but he knew. There was no invitation in the words, not even an invitation in her eyes. But he knew.

She turned to camera 2, seducing America as effectively as she had seduced him.

He smiled, a little too confident, a little too male, a little too sexually charged, but he couldn't help it.

Something had happened twelve months ago. A flash of lightning, a magnetic pull. And for twelve months it had stayed buried. But no more. Tonight they were going to finish it.

MERCEDES GOT UP ON WOBBLY legs, parts of her swelling that shouldn't be swelling under the hot lights of the television cameras. She gave Sam a wobbly smile.

"You did good."

"It was fun. I thought I was going to be nervous. I was nervous. Hell, I was terrified, but then it got fun."

"I'm glad," he answered softly. She loved his voice, the smoothness, the power, the comfort. She wanted to say something witty and seductive, but her synapses were as overloaded as she was. She needed to leave, run away, and turn back into the confident, successful person that she was supposed to be. She started to go.

"Mercedes?"

She turned, looked at him, and saw the heat in his eyes. "Yeah?" she squeaked.

"You free for dinner? It's a tradition here on the show."

Oh, that was a nice touch. Make it look like it was merely business. Nothing more than a polite gesture. "I'd love to. All that talking and I'm suddenly hungry."

This time she did leave, walking unsteadily into the waiting room, her teeth chattering from the air conditioned cold. Her fingers tapped on her knees as she contemplated the depth of her over-the-headness. Sam Porter was no Andreas. Sam Porter was no plaything. He was all man, and tonight she was going to hear that seductive voice whispering heady, seduce-me words against her neck. Tonight she was going to feel that big body thrusting inside her. A moan escaped her lips, with only the clock as a witness.

Tick. Tick. Tick.

THEY HAD DINNER AT Fisherman's Wharf, at a seafood restaurant perched on a dock that reached out far into the bay. It was dark, warm, and intimate, much nicer than the waiting room at the television studio. This was a place a man took a date for privacy and romance. Across the way, the moon lit up the island prison of Alcatraz, giving it a ghostly glow. This was a place that Mercedes would write about in her book.

Sam was a wonderful companion, telling her stories about his guests, making her laugh all the way through dinner. His eyes lit up as he talked, and she could see how much he loved what he did, how passionate he was about his work.

She liked that about him, his passion. So many people punched a clock, and didn't care, but Sam cared. It was there in his words, his face, in the intensity that radiated from him.

It was that intensity that drew her like a magnet.

"So what've you been doing for the past twelve months—besides writing a book?"

"Not a lot. This. That."

"Nothing else to keep you busy? No personal obligations, huh?"

"Are you asking if I'm involved?" she said, meeting his eyes squarely. Mercedes had never been one to tiptoe around something; she wanted people to know she was coming.

One side of his mouth curved up, a rueful look that

shouldn't have touched her like it did. Mercedes knew her way around men, she knew her way up, down, and four-way sideways. She didn't trust them as a rule, but that small hitch in his mouth tempted her to bend her rules. Just a little.

"Yeah, that's what I'm asking," he said, surprising her with his honesty.

"Free as a bird," she answered easily, her tone light.

He nodded once, only once, a supremely male nod of satisfaction, and her stomach knotted, excitement and nerves all pitching together into one tangle. She pushed the hair from her eyes with a shaking hand. It was sex.

Just sex. The one reason she had flown across the country was because she wanted him. Even after twelve months, that ache hadn't eased, it ate at her, pouring into her fantasies, her dreams, her writing, turning into something living, breathing inside her. Something more.

Abruptly she pushed that thought away, needing to regain her footing. "Thank you for asking me to dinner."

He leaned in closer, the candlelight touching off the tawny streaks in his hair. "Don't thank me, Mercedes. I really don't deserve it."

"This bothers you, doesn't it?"

He laughed, a rusty sound without humor. "You have no idea how much."

She flashed him her best smile. "Yeah, I think I do."

She watched as he deftly made patterns with the last of the silverware, and was pleased to see him uncomfortable, pleased to know she wasn't the only one whose nerves were shot to hell. Finally he raised his head, his jaw tight. "I didn't plan to have this conversation over dinner."

"Is there a right time and a right place, Sam?"

His eyes glittered, more brown than green in the dim light, his desire apparent. Mercedes shifted in her seat, trapping the pulse between her thighs. "Yes," he said harshly, his carefully modulated television voice now gone.

Mercedes smiled. "In bed."

"Preferably before then."

"Maybe I like to know what I'm getting into."

"Mercedes," he started, then stopped. "No. Would you like some dessert?"

"What's on the menu?" she asked.

He closed his eyes. "Are you going to behave?"

"Dinner was your idea, not mine."

He pulled some cash from his pocket and laid it on the table. "Can we go?"

"*Now* we're in a hurry?" she asked.

He lifted their jackets from the coat hook at the table. "Dinner was a stupid idea. In a long line of stupid ideas. But I've waited twelve months, and right now, every minute counts."

Mercedes felt a sharp pull of excitement in her stomach. He held out her jacket, and she backed against him. Closer than she should. Close enough to brush against him. Close enough to feel him jutting thickly against her bottom. Close enough to hear his indrawn breath.

"I guess you're ready?" she asked.

He swore softly, took her arm, and hurried her out of the place.

HE DROVE HER BACK TO THE hotel in silence. What did you say to a man you were about to step off the cliff with? They walked through the lobby, and he was careful not to touch her, but she could feel him, feel the invisible band of awareness between them, arching like an electrical shock. A few fans recognized him in the lobby, and stopped to talk about the show, and she stood discreetly off to the side, not knowing what else to do. The etiquette books didn't cover this situation.

After he finished talking, he put a hand in the small of her back and guided her to the bank of elevators. "Do you get accosted by fans very often?"

"Not a lot," he answered, but she suspected that was wrong.

"I bet when you go to Kansas, you're mobbed with screaming females."

"I have male fans, too," he said. Ah, she'd struck a nerve.

"Do they scream and throw underwear at you?"

"No one has ever thrown underwear at me."

"Got them in the mail, huh?"

His face flushed. "A couple of times."

"I'll remember that," she said, as they stepped into the elevator. "It's your green eyes. Very sexy."

"I have hazel eyes."

"Whatever you say, Sam."

They were quiet on the ride to the ninth floor and she noted that he didn't even ask what floor she was on. Somewhere along the line, she had given him an answer.

He was so controlled, so careful as they walked down the hallway, but the heat was coming off him in waves. His strides got a little longer, and she noticed that his breathing wasn't completely even. Somebody was completely turned on.

Somebody besides her.

He took out his key, glanced down the hallway, and then escorted her inside his suite.

And that was the end of his control.

4

SAM HAULED HER BACK against the door, and crushed his mouth to hers, and Mercedes heard herself whimper. Two parts relief and one part fear. This wasn't a book, this was her life, and right at the moment she wasn't sure she could breathe. His body was so tight against hers that she could feel the pulse of his blood, the beat of his heart, the fierce jerk of his cock. She opened her legs, cradling him there, feeling him rub against her. It was the most erotic thing she'd ever felt, which, for a writer of erotica, was saying quite a lot.

His lips moved against her throat, nuzzling against her neck, and then he began to murmur. All those soft, seductive words that she had dreamed, fantasized about hearing. And Mr. Conservative had a wicked, wicked tongue.

"Tell me you're okay with this, Mercedes," he muttered.

Ah, man, she was so much more than okay with this. His hands swept over her breasts, along her hips, underneath her dress, and all she could do was nod.

He shoved aside the neck of her dress, and his mouth fastened on her breast. The pain was sharp, fierce, and she gasped with the intensity of it. Then with his tongue, he warmed where he hurt, pulling, laving, arrowing mindless shivers of heat to her nipples, and liquid tears between her thighs.

Weakly, her head fell back against the wall, her knees buckling. He took her in his arms, and carried her over to the couch, and before she could regain any control, he was on her again.

It was heaven, the heavy weight of him a welcome torment. He shoved up her dress, he unzipped his pants, and then, oh, glory, he was inside her.

His thrusts were hard, thick, and it took a few strokes for her to adjust, but then her body took over, the exquisite feeling of completeness filled her, and she rose up to meet him. His mouth covered hers, his tongue thrusting in time with their bodies, and her fingernails dug into his shoulder, holding on tightly.

The air of the hotel grew heavy with the scent of sex, the sound of their breathing, the smacking of flesh against flesh. All she could think was that this was Sam. *Sam.*

For twelve months, she had dreamed, but never like this. This wasn't hazy or warm, this cut inside her, sharper than a knife. Her fingers lost their hold, and she gave herself up to the orgasm, jumping off the cliff, right into the air.

His thrusts went deep to her core, and she could feel the world falling away.

SAM'S CHEST WAS RACING, and he wondered if he would have a heart attack. Surely not, he was in great shape, but he felt like he'd just knocked two decades off his life.

Mercedes. She was going to kill him. But at least he'd die happy. He considered pulling out of the soft, vibrant body beneath him, but he couldn't do that, not yet. It was so comfortable to lay here, his head pillowed against her breasts, listening to her heart. For two beats he stayed still, his breath slowing to match hers.

However, Sam had been raised as a gentleman, and gentlemen didn't lie there like a one hundred and ninety-pound slug. But he needed to know the answers to the questions he'd kept inside for so long. He lifted his head, met her eyes, wanting to know what secrets her eyes held when a man was inside her.

There. He looked there, and was dazzled. She would never be a woman with stars in her eyes; she was too alive, too passionate. But a man could still fall into the darkness. Drown in the sparks of joy and life that even the darkness couldn't hide.

Now he knew. This obsession should be over. He should be satisfied, ready to go out, buy his cherry-red sports car, and learn to play golf. Instead, his cock forgot that he was approaching mid-life; it was fat, happy, and ready to go again. Did a man really need a sports car? Probably not.

He raised his hips, ready to start all over, when those passionate eyes widened with panic. "A condom," she said, the words coming out in a rush.

Shit, shit, shit, shit. Sam took a deep breath. He was the older, more responsible party, he could handle this. "Okay, we're going to run through the checklist. I'm clean. You?"

She nodded.

"Pregnancy?" he asked, his mind seeing Mercedes rounded with child. His child.

"I'm on the pill," she answered quickly, and he wiped the image from his brain.

This time, Sam did pull out of her, and then sat up on the couch. "I'm sorry."

"S'all right," she answered, all the sparkle gone from her face. Somehow reality had intruded, and stole all the happiness from her. She pinned up her hair, and then began to pull her clothes together to cover her body, a crime against humanity, if there ever was one.

He took her hands. "Mercedes, stop." She looked up at him, regret in her eyes. He'd been an ass. They were going to start over, and this time, he was going to seduce her right.

SEX HAD NEVER BEEN THE highlight of Mercedes's life. It was good enough, sure, but afterward, there was always an afterward. In that afterward, she never knew how to act, how not to act, or what to say, and her choice of lovers had been no help.

As she fumbled with her clothes, Sam stilled her hands, and she froze. She didn't want to meet his eyes, didn't want to see apathy there, but she had always been a sucker for pain, so she looked. No apathy, not today. This was something else not usually seen in the face of her lovers. Comfort, rock-like determination, and strength.

He gave her a half-smile and told her to stop. Obediently she stopped, because this was new and different. No one ever gave her instructions before.

"Please stay," he asked huskily. "Just tonight."

Just tonight. One night of sex. It seemed fitting for them. Their whole relationship—although "relationship" was an overstatement—was built on the sliding bedrock of sex. The subject of sex, nerve-shattering sexual attraction, debating the effect of sex on America.

He wasn't offering anything more. And she didn't want anything more. Right?

So one night, just one night, would be absolutely perfect.

Numbly she nodded. He took her hand and led her through the suite to the bedroom.

Sam pulled her into his arms, lowered his head, and kissed her. It wasn't like earlier, this was soft as a cloud, and gentle. He played with her lips, easing into the kiss, using his tongue, not as a weapon, but as a toy. Harmless, teasing, seductive. This wasn't the hot fire of sex, this was a slow warmth, two people melting into one.

Mercedes kissed him back, winding her arms around his neck, moving closer to his warmth. She shivered once, and he lifted his head.

"Cold?"

"A little," she lied. Actually, she was terrified. Sex didn't scare her, but this new aspect, this thing beyond seduction, did.

"Easily fixed," he said, his voice as soft and gentle as his kiss. "Stay here for a minute."

He left her, and she stood, arms wrapped around her stomach. For the first time she noticed the luxury of her surroundings. The huge bed covered in a plump down duvet and piles of pillows. A flat screen TV hung on the wall, flanked by large bouquets of fresh flowers. The brocade curtains were open to the city, and in the night a constellation of lights blinked from the buildings and houses below.

She rubbed her arms, feeling the cold, the loneliness, and wondered what was wrong with her.

Sam returned, took her hand and pulled her in the

bathroom. "You look like you've been hit by a truck," he said.

Mercedes laughed nervously. "I feel like that."

"It's been a long day for you. The jet lag, attack of nerves, and I haven't helped. Let me take care of you, huh?"

His explanation made sense. She wasn't scared. She was tired. It'd been a long day. That must be it. "Sounds great," she said, eyeing the bath in the corner. It was huge, a raised square that seated four comfortably.

"You want some wine, whiskey, water?"

"Whiskey."

He went off, came back with a neat glass of whiskey, no ice. It was exactly what she needed, something to settle her nerves, bring back the confidence that she was currently sorely lacking. She took a long swallow, feeling the burn in her throat.

"Better?"

"Yes, thanks."

"You want me to come back when you're done?"

Again with the gentleness, again she felt the rock of fear inside her. She didn't want gentleness, she craved the white heat of passion. Somehow the whiskey and the look in his eyes were doing a number on her normal, independent nature. "Please stay," she said, mainly because she had no choice.

"You're sure?"

She nodded, and reached around to unzip her dress.

He stopped her hands once again. "No."

He dimmed the lights, lit the candles next to the sink, the flames flickering in the mirror. "I should have thought. I'm no good at this, Mercedes."

"I'm not complaining," she said, as he came to stand next to her.

He kissed her once. Lightly. Then he turned her around, and slowly unzipped her dress, the cold air tickling her spine as her bare back was exposed. Sam slid the dress off one shoulder, then the other, before it pooled at her feet. His hands grasped her shoulders, and he placed a kiss against the sensitive spot at the nape of her neck. She shivered again, not from cold, but from heat. He cupped her breasts in his hand and pulled her back against him. "You don't know how beautiful you are, do you?"

The sound of his voice, hard, and not nearly gentle, shocked her nearly as much as the words. "I'm okay," she answered.

He turned her around to face him, and her hands rose to cover her breasts.

"I thought you were an empowered, sexually liberated woman," he teased.

"I am," she said, her hands still glued to her breasts.

"Ah, Mercedes, what am I going to do with you?"

Then he kissed her again, this time not so softly. Her hands fell away, which she suspected was his plan all along, but she couldn't deny the urge to feel her bare skin against his—shirt? No. The white-heat returned, the familiar territory of sex. This place she knew. Quickly she attacked the buttons, divesting him of the thing. This time when he kissed her, the fear was gone. Dark hair covered his chest, crisp and curling, and when he held her against him, it teased her nipples, and she knew she couldn't date a man without chest hair ever. Sam had ruined it for her.

His mouth moved from her lips to her throat, and lei-
surely he tasted the skin there. Her head tilted back,
reveling in the heady luxury of simply being kissed.
The passion cooled, the warmth returned, but it was
easier now. It was like a dream to her, the dreams that
had filled her head. The scent of the flowers against the
musky scent of his cologne, the feel of his hands
soothing her flesh, soothing her. The taste of his kiss lingering in her mouth.

It was all so nice, so relaxing. So easy.

His hands cupped her rear, skimming her flesh, and
then, with a magician's touch, her panties were gone.
There she stood, clad in her thigh-highs and heels and
nothing else, but she was no longer cold or nervous. The
heat of the bath, the heat of his hands had warmed her.
He lifted her on the counter and bent to slip off her
shoes. As the shoes hit the marble floor, the sound
echoed in the quiet, but Mercedes was too content to
care, drunk on something far more potent than whiskey.
Sam raised her legs, bending her knees, her feet
balanced on the counter. His fingers slid under the edge
of one stocking and rolled it slowly down her leg. His
hands lingered, touching, caressing, always soft and
gentle, always safe. When he was done, he lifted her
from the counter, and eased her into the bath, her
muscles flowing like liquid.

"There," he said. "Close your eyes, Mercedes."

She followed his instructions and leaned her head
back against the wall of the tub. She heard the rustle of
his clothes, and she smiled. How did he know she loved
baths? Did he guess, could he read her mind? She didn't
know, didn't care. When she felt the strength of his

body behind her, sheltering her, she wondered why they had wasted twelve months getting to this point. He was perfect.

Never before had she appreciated the yin and yang of the human form, the hard male a fitting contradiction to the softness of the female. Two opposites joining together as one. In so many ways they were different, but here, at the very basic level, it worked. Sam took the washcloth and lathered soap over her back, her shoulders, letting the warm water dribble over her, and Mercedes sighed, resting her head on his chest.

"This is nice," she murmured.

"I'm glad to see you coming back to life." The velvet voice rumbled, vibrating against her spine. He was lulling her even further, seducing her to the place where real emotion resided. It would be so easy to drift there, but this wasn't about emotion. This was about sex.

Just one night.

She wiggled against him, feeling his erection pressing against her rear. "I'm not the only one."

"There's time enough. Relax."

"Sex is very relaxing," she argued.

"I didn't want to jump on you again, Mercedes. I wanted to seduce you."

He lingered over the words, luring her into dangerous waters, much more tempting than the bath itself. She resisted his siren's call, and shifted to face him, straddling her legs over his. "I'm seduced. Tell me you already put on a condom."

"Yeah."

"So all that bit about not wanting to jump me?"

"Mercedes, I will always want to jump you."

She laughed and inched forward, until his cock was brushing against her nether lips and Sam closed his eyes, breathing in deeply.

"Good?" she asked, her sanity returning.

"You're too much for me, Mercedes."

She moved again, impaling herself on him. Slowly she rose, a quiet splash of the water as she slid upwards, his cock sliding out. As she moved, she watched his face, her gaze tracing the ever-changing colors of his eyes, the controlled line of his jaw, the rise and fall of his broad chest. She could feel the blood quickening through her veins, sharp and brilliant, her senses beginning to simmer once again.

She slid down, his thickness filling her. This is what she craved, letting the heat burn her. His hands rose to cup her breasts, his thumbs brushing against her nipples. Her gaze locked with his and she kept up her rhythm, moving up and down on him. For a good bit, he let her, but then his eyes grew sharper, as he felt the fire, too. The next time she lifted herself, he turned her, her breasts pressed against the edge of the tub, and roughly pushed inside her from behind. She had thought she had control, but no longer. Sam had taken over, and she could only follow his lead.

He cradled her body, and then reached beyond her, pressing a button next to the tub. Jets whirled to life, sending water cascading in circles around them. He pressed a hand in the valley between her thighs, parting her thighs, parting her swollen lips, until the pulsing water swirled her.

It was like an explosion inside her. Sam filling her from behind, the water an added gentle pressure, and she couldn't think. His finger worked her over, and each time she moaned, he only thrust inside harder and faster.

Time stopped, the world spun, Mercedes heard her cries, and this time, Sam caught her before she fell.

5

THEY LAY IN BED, SAM stroking her silky hair. He felt like a teenager again, his body sated yet energized. Mercedes curled up against him, where she belonged, her eyes drifting closed as she fought sleep.

Sam pressed a kiss against her forehead.

"If I die tonight, I think I should tell you where my important documents are."

One eye opened and she looked at him. "Why are you telling me this? You aren't going to die. That's incredibly morbid."

"I'm older than you, Mercedes. It could happen." Especially if he kept making love to her like a fifteen-year-old.

"You're not that much older than me, Sam."

"Twenty years is a lot older."

She raised up on her elbow and looked at him. "You are the hottest forty-six-year-old man I've ever met."

He did the math, and then looked at her carefully. "You're twenty-six?"

"Yes. How old did you think I was?"

"Twenty-one. Eighteen. It didn't matter. You're too young."

"Oh, come on. You sound like it's perverted or something. I've been living on my own for eight years now.

I understand the concepts of laundry and paying bills, and how to hold down a steady job, albeit not for very often. I can drink alcohol, and even vote."

He pushed a hand through his hair, considering these new facts before him. "Twenty-six?"

"Want to see my ID?"

"No. You're really twenty-six?"

"This is freaking you out, isn't it?"

"I don't act like this, Mercedes."

"Like what?"

"Like something out of your book."

"I thought you didn't read it."

"Maybe some."

She whapped him on the chest. "Sam Porter, you lied. You so read my stuff." Her mouth shifted into a frown. "Is that why we're here? Is it my writing or me?"

He swept a hand over her, contemplating the willowy curves of the twenty-six-year-old body. "You write hot stuff, yes, but you fired my engines way before I read your book."

"Why didn't you ask me out then?"

"You have a habit of putting personal liaisons into your blog for public consumption. That's not me. I like my private life private."

"You aren't nervous now?"

"Are you going to put anything out there?" he asked, careful to keep any emotion out of his voice. He didn't exactly trust her, but that barn door was open, and the cows were smoking post-coital cigarettes in somebody else's pasture.

"No."

"See? No problem there."

"You really read my book?"

"Yeah."

"Did you like it?"

"It certainly involved me physically."

"But did you like it?" she pressed.

Sam knew the verbal minefield she was laying before him. He was a master of the technique. "You'll only get mad if I answer this question."

"No, I won't."

"Yes, you will."

"No, I won't."

"Okay, it's not my thing. It's hot, very arousing, but I'm not into emotional reads."

"Fine," she said, sounding mad.

"You're mad."

"I'm not mad," she snapped.

"You're mad. I told you, you'd get mad."

"If you have no concept of the emotional and sexual reaches of two people, then you have no taste, and I refuse to let someone who has no taste make me mad."

"Oh come on, Mercedes. I'm a guy. That stuff isn't for me."

"You're sexist."

"No, biologically, men and woman are different. Our bodies, our minds. I didn't invent that."

"That's an incredibly old-fashioned attitude."

"I'm an incredibly old-fashioned man."

She lifted an eyebrow. "Not that old-fashioned, honey. That wasn't the missionary position you were using back there."

"Man, tell me about it. I could've thrown out my back."

Mercedes smiled, and he forgot about his back.

"Tell me about you. I know all about how you feel about fiscal responsibility, prayer in public schools, and the governor of New Jersey, but I have no idea about your life." She paused. "You're not married, are you?"

"No. Divorced a long time ago."

"Back in the stone ages?"

"Stop."

"You asked for it. Tell me something else. What do you do when you're not working?"

"I like to fish. I have a cabin upstate I go to sometimes to relax. Take Max up there, listen to silence."

"Max?"

"Dog. Have you ever been fishing?"

"Nah. It's too slow for me. Too quiet. I'm used to the noise of the city. If the world gets quiet, then something is wrong. When it's loud, cars honking, music blaring, everything is safe."

"So that's why you became a writer. Because it's such a noisy occupation."

She looked at him, slightly bemused. "I don't know. When did you decide you wanted to be on TV?"

"I didn't. My agent did. I was a journalist in Pennsylvania, and I did some of the local news. The network saw my work and liked it."

"I think it's cool. Having that much attention, being in the spotlight."

"For fifteen minutes, maybe. But after that, it's like being the only goldfish in one of those tiny bowls. You really want fame, huh?"

"For at least fifteen minutes. Just to know. Andrew's famous in the financial circles, he hates it. Sheldon's famous in the tabloids, she hates it. I'd like to experience it, so I could decide, and possibly hate it, for myself."

"Be careful what you wish for, Mercedes. What does it matter if you're famous or not?"

"Everyone loves you when you're famous. It proves to the world that you're worthy. You're somebody."

"You're somebody already."

"Not to everybody."

"Who's everybody?"

"Are you trying to psychoanalyze me?"

"No, I'm trying to understand what you're saying."

"I thought I was very clear."

"You were cryptic, not clear."

"That wasn't cryptic."

"Then who's everybody, Miss I'm Not Cryptic?"

"Nobody."

"See? You proved my point. You're cryptic."

She pulled up the sheet, burrowed into the pillows, almost disappearing. "Did you know your father?" she asked in a tiny voice.

"Yeah. Nobody's influenced me more."

"I didn't know mine. Mom says he's a good-for-nothing son-of-a-bitch. I want to be something. Something that makes the papers. Something that makes him turn to the *New York Times,* or *Newsweek,* or even the Sam Porter show, and see me, his daughter. Watch me. Realize what he walked away from. If I'm not famous, he'll never know me."

Sam followed her into the blankets, wanting to hold her. His arms slid around her and he wished he could meet the man who had hurt her so badly, but all he could do was talk. "Your father was a jerk.

You're shaping your whole life around someone that shouldn't matter."

"He doesn't matter to me," she answered, all bravado, most likely fake. "I don't think about him enough that it can bother me. He left us, that's ancient history. I just want him to know. I want him to feel bad for what he's done. And that's why I want to be famous."

She grew quiet then, and Sam didn't press her anymore. She had so many things that she wanted to prove to the world, and Sam didn't have the heart to tell her that life didn't work that way. You played with the cards you were dealt. She fell asleep, dreaming of the world she wanted to conquer, while Sam lay awake, staring at the ceiling, sad that somewhere along the way, he'd lost the all-consuming fire of his youth.

MERCEDES WOKE TO THE sound of Sam's voice. At first she thought someone else was in the hotel room, but his was the only voice she heard. He was on the phone.

She slipped out of bed, pulled on the thick, fluffy robe, and opened the curtains, letting the sun warm her face. Last night it had been so easy to get carried away on the fantasy, but in five hours she would be on a flight back to New York, hopefully seated next to someone other than McCreepy.

This was the afterwards she had dreaded, only Sam had gotten the timeline all screwed up. Oh, well. She knew the drill.

She dressed in a hurry, finding her clothes stacked neatly in a chair. How did she know he wasn't a slob? After a check in the mirror, a fluff of her hair, and a dab at the mascara smudged on her cheek, she looked full of confidence, and ready to face the world. Or at least him.

She practiced her smile, and then listened outside the bedroom door, making sure no one else was around. Satisfied, she took one deep breath and entered the main room of the suite.

"Good morning," she chirped, sounding like an actress in an orange juice commercial. He had pulled on a pair of jeans, and an old flannel shirt hung open. Two newspapers were spread out in front of him, CNN was on TV, and there was a cup of coffee by his side. He looked like an average American male. So why did her heart go bump?

No, just one night. She was going to leave, and put everything behind her. "I wanted to pick up my purse, and I'll be off."

He rose, stuffed his hands in his pockets. "Did Kristin arrange for a car to take you to the airport?"

"Oh, yeah. Got that covered. We're not in the middle of nowhere."

"Mercedes?"

"Yeah, Sam?"

She could see the confusion in his face, in those marvelous hazel eyes, and understood. Theirs was a relationship based on lust and nothing more. He was fun and chatty, and told good stories, but he wasn't for her. No, Sam deserved someone less flighty, less self-centered, probably someone who did charity work or taught school, and certainly didn't spend two days picking out the perfect pair of shoes.

Not every story had a happy ending. She gave him her most mature smile. "See you around, huh?"

"Yeah."

Then she walked out on her fabulous Jimmy Choo sandals, leaving Sam Porter, and one night of life-altering sex behind.

6

FOR THE NEXT FEW DAYS, Mercedes padded around her apartment, trying to ignore her silent phone. It wasn't easy. They were ships who happened to pass through San Francisco on the same night, in the same bed. It'd been great, a chance to do something that would happen in her books, but now it was history. It all sounded really good, but didn't help ease the empty spot inside her.

When the phone finally did ring, she told herself it wasn't Sam, and miracle of miracles, it wasn't. Jamie had called about dressing fittings (oh, joy), and her mother reminded her about Sunday dinner (Mercedes pleaded jet lag, and begged off).

She didn't want to face her family. Didn't want to see Sheldon happily in love with Jeff. Or Andrew and Jamie, who weren't nearly as silly as Sheldon and Jeff, but every now and then Mercedes would catch them staring at each other, and felt like a person on a galaxy far, far away.

Everyone had someone but Mercedes, and on most days that didn't bother her, but right now, it stung.

Monday morning dawned in the Big Apple after several long, sleepless nights, and her agent called and asked her to meet her for drinks at Michael's restaurant.

Drinks with her agent. Now *that* should cheer her up. Mercedes wasn't cheered.

On a good day, Michael's was the be-all, end-all for the literati. The A-list book people got the tables near the window, and the little guppies got the tables in the back. The host showed Mercedes to a table near the front. Okay, things were looking up.

Portia McLarin was the perfect literary agent. Tall, New York slender (possibly size 2), always dressed in designer black, with these big round tortoise-shell glasses to signify her smarts. She hung up and looked at Mercedes over her glasses.

Normally, Portia's mouth was compressed into a tight line; today, it was so tightly compressed, it totally disappeared from her face.

And when Portia wasn't happy, Mercedes was even unhappier. "Did you see the show last week?" she asked, trying for a smile.

Portia's mouth appeared again. "Yeah, you were good. Sparks. Definitely sparks, and I'm sure you moved some merchandise."

"Always a good thing, right?"

Portia nodded once. Not a good thing. Once the drinks were on the table, Portia got to the black heart of the matter. "I've got some bad news."

"Go ahead," answered Mercedes.

"Look, doll, I don't know exactly what happened here, or who dropped the ball, but we need to perform triage on your sales efforts."

"My sales efforts?"

"Mm-huh. Something to give them a boost, bring your name to the forefront. Got any ideas?"

Sure. Just slept with conservative talk show host, Sam Porter. Had wild, wonderful sex that meant absolutely nothing to him. And meant nothing to her, too, she reminded herself. Other than that, not so much. "Portia, I'm not sure exactly what I can do. The book is already on the shelves now."

"I know. If that whoremonger of an actress hadn't published her memoirs at the same time as your book hit, we wouldn't be having this conversation. I tell you, it's always something. What about your blog? Got any juicy stories, or rumors? What about your sister-in-law?"

Mercedes sipped at her cosmopolitan, which was going down like battery acid. "I can talk to Sheldon, but she's not exactly in the spotlight anymore."

"Oh, such a waste. All that fame—poof."

"I'll find something, Portia. I can write some new stuff for the blog. Pure fiction. No gossip, just some stories."

"That would be good. Freebies. People always like freebies."

"I'll post something tomorrow," she promised.

"Oh, wait. I do have some good news!"

Well, Hallelujah. Mercedes managed a smile. "Good news would be good."

Portia grabbed her glorious Hermes bag from the floor and rummaged through the buttery-soft goatskin leather interior. Eventually Portia pulled out an envelope and handed it over. "Got this today from your ed. Fan mail, doll. Get used to it."

Mercedes stared at the simple white envelope. Okay, her personal life was a wreck, her career was in the dump, but oh my god, a fan letter. A concrete affirmation of her life-long dreams to be a famous writer. Portia jabbed scarlet-tipped nails in her direction. "Go on, don't leave us hanging. Open it!"

Mercedes bit her lip, torn between a genuine desire to find something uplifting in her life, and fear that this was another thunderbolt from the gods. "But what if they hate me? What if it's a listing of every typographical error ever known to man, or a dissertation on the various tenses of the word 'lay'?"

"Should I read it for you?"

"Please," Mercedes said, happy to have the choice taken away from her.

Using her talons like a letter-opener, Portia ripped into the paper and pulled out a single type-written sheet of paper.

"Dear Ms. Brooks, I wanted to compliment you on your debut work. It is very rare that an author can convey such an intimate look at erotic behaviors with such finesse, capturing the subtle nuances such as the feel, smell and taste of a man.

You have a new fan, and I look forward to discovering your next work of erotica.

Yours, Jane in Rhode Island."

"Look at that! Jane in Rhode Island. A new fan."

Mercedes gazed in awe at the sanitized courier font, the plain sheet of paper, and smiled a big smile. Okay, maybe the day was getting better after all. Just a little bit.

SAM GOT UP EARLY ON Tuesday, earlier than usual, mainly because he hadn't slept. He considered going back to bed, but it was almost 9:00 a.m., and if he really believed everything he told America on a nightly basis, he should be working.

He started to make notes on the senate race in Minnesota, and instead made up notes of what he wanted to tell Mercedes.

Say Hello.

How was the flight back?

Sam's a jerk.

Sam's an old jerk.

Sam has a recliner. Does this bother you? You probably don't like recliners, do you? You probably have a modern white couch, uncomfortable as hell, and if Max jumped up on it, which he would because he's not very well-behaved, you'd have black dog hair all over it. You're allergic to dogs, aren't you?

He sighed, and threw the paper in the trash.

Work was the last thing he wanted to do right now, but he didn't have a choice. Except for the one favor he needed to take care of first. He called Franco, his ex-business manager, who never rolled out of bed before noon, and woke him up. What were friends for?

"Yeah, sorry about the early call, but this is important. I have a friend who needs to climb back into the wonderful world of women, and I want to take him someplace where he can meet lots of babes. Easy. Low-stress, ego-enhancing atmosphere."

"Is he cool?" mumbled Franco.

"Average."

"Good average or bad average?"

Sam thought for a minute. "Good average."

"You should hire a wing lady."

"What?"

"A wing lady. It used to be a wing man, but now the ladies are doing it, too. You get a hot lady to come out with the guys and she'll bring the traffic in his direction. Works like a babe-magnet."

"That's more Machiavellian than I was hoping for. I could just bring a date." Mercedes would like a club. He could ask her out. And he would be helping Tony out, too. Mercedes would do that. Help out a friend of Sam's. Assuming that she was still speaking to Sam.

"No dates, my friend. Big mistake. *Big. Mistake.* Then you have complications. Expectations. Tribulations. And finally—commiserations."

"This is not a contract negotiation, Franco."

"I know, a contract negotiation involves much less blood."

"Just give me a place to go."

"Trident."

"Where's it at?"

"Lower East Side."

"Not the Meatpacking District?"

"That's passé. L.E.S. is where stuff's happening."

"Okay," he said, writing it down. "Hey, got something I want to run by you."

"At nine in the morning? Can't it wait?"

"Yeah, it can wait."

Silence. "Okay, what is it?"

"Do you think I'd be good at politics?"

Franco laughed, which was, in a way, an answer. Not the answer Sam was hoping for, but an answer. "Why do you want to torture yourself?"

"It wouldn't be torture. I might do some good."

"Sure, if you were Jimmy Stewart, and the year was 1940. In this day and age, you'll get raked over the coals. Political operatives will be combing through your trash to find something to use on you, and lobbyists'll be sending you to golf courses in Scotland and asking you to build polar bear museums in Atlanta."

"You're making this up to scare me."

"The polar bear museum is true."

"So this would be a bad thing?"

"Yes. The absolute worst."

"You're right," Sam agreed. "Definitely not smart. You want to head out with us when we hit the club?"

"Can't. I'm responsible for cooking dinner."

"Cook? Isn't that a four-letter word for you?"

"Mandy."

"Mandy?"

"Mandy."

"I don't talk to you for two days and you're cooking dinner for a female? What happened to the whole 'women as a fruit orchard' mentality? Remember that, moving from tree to tree, sampling their fruit, drunk on their nectar? That was you who said that, wasn't it?"

"Mandy's nice. She goes to Columbia."

"How old is Mandy?"

"Twenty-eight."

Sam groaned. "I feel like I'm a dying breed, Franco. A dinosaur among men."

"You *are* getting old, Sam."

"Don't say that. Thirty-nine is not old."

"Thirty-nine is old."

"It's too early for this much depression. I'm hanging up, Franco. Trident, right?"

"Yeah. And hire a wing lady. I know a service, if you need a number."

"Goodbye, Franco. I can find a woman all by myself. Even if I am old."

With that, Sam hung up and pulled his notes from the trash can.

She knew that he wasn't her perfect man. Her perfect man didn't exist, but this one, this one with the placid green eyes that were marked with crinkles at the corner. He was strong, his body long and lean, with muscles that didn't come from the gym, but from the outdoors. His face showed lines of wisdom and character, the brown hair touched with gold from so many hours in the sun. He was the man you wanted with you in troubled times; he was the man you wanted with you in bed.

He captured her thoughts and her desires in a way that she'd never expected. She'd never made love to him before, but she could imagine him lying over her, covering her with his hard length, his cock thrusting inside her slowly. He would be slow, methodical, patient, she knew. Everything he did was slow and methodical. She hummed to herself, already anticipating the time that she knew would come soon.

She dressed for their date carefully. It wasn't supposed to be a date; after all, they were nothing more than friends. He thought he was too old for her, she knew better, and tonight she would seduce him and let him realize he was wrong. It would be her pleasure. He showed up at her door, and she'd decided to greet him in her robe.

"You're early," she said, watching as his gaze swept over her, feeling each touch.

"I'm on time," he answered, but she noticed the catch in his voice and she heard the edge of his need lingering there as well.

"Wow, I must be running late. Come on in, I'll finish getting dressed." She kept her eyes downcast, hiding her hunger from him. It was too soon, and he wouldn't want to be chased. He was the hunter, and tonight, she would be his prey.

He sat on her couch, waiting patiently, but she ached to do something to jar him out of his placid calm. She went into her bedroom, leaving the door open and slipped the robe from her shoulders, watching him from the mirror in her room.

He gazed at her quietly, not moving, but the air was thicker than before, more heated, and she could feel the swelling in the flesh between her thighs.

She reached into her closet, finding the dress she had intended to wear, laying her bra, panties and hose on the bed.

Egged on by some mysterious spark, she ignored the bra and panties, and went straight for the hose. She sat on the side of the bed, and rolled on the thigh-high hose, slow, seductively, a strip tease in reverse. Still he watched, and even from here she could see the pulse ticking in the side of his jaw. Good.

She pulled her heels from under the bed, and crossed one leg over the other, *Basic Instinct* style. With shaking fingers, she struggled with the tiny buckle, and she wondered where was her poise, her confidence?

When she looked up, he stood over her.

"Here, let me help," he answered. He bent beside the bed, his hands sliding down her thigh, down her calf to cradle her foot. His fingers were careful and efficient, sliding the buckle home, and he repeated the procedure with the other foot.

Her heart was pounding with awareness as he stood, towering over her and slowly he pushed her back against the bed, parting her thighs. His fingers, still careful and efficient, caressed the agitated flesh, soothing it, melting her until she was damp with need. He didn't say anything, only watched her with his heavy-lidded gaze as he played with her, pleasuring her. Her hips lifted toward his hand, giving him easier access to the hidden places inside her. She sighed with delight, her body dancing in time with the slow waltz that he was leading. Then he removed his hand and she frowned, wondering what she'd done wrong. He sat down on the bed next to her and took the silky thong she had planned on wearing. He lifted her hands over her head and used the fabric to knot her hands to the bed. She looked at him, surprised, but he was implacable, his eyes drifting over her supple body, and she wished she could read his mind. Wished she knew what pleasured him. He was a quiet man of few words, and seeing this secret part of him touched her heart.

He left her tied to the bed, and then returned shortly, bearing a store of her treasures.

She smiled in delight as he opened up the bottle of chocolate. Carefully he drizzled it over her beaded nipples, down her stomach, between her thighs. She would have to launder her sheets tomorrow, but tonight she would live like the gods.

The bed creaked under his weight, as he lay down next to her. She tensed, waiting, and then his head bent to her breast, his tongue flicking against one nipple, laving her skin, cleaning the chocolate from her. Her body squirmed with delight, her back arching to move closer to him. Next he turned to the other breast and tasted her again. With each stroke of his tongue, she pulled harder against the silken bonds that held her, the torture exquisite.

He followed the mocha trail down her body with his lips, leaving prickles of excitement in his wake. The hard stubble on his jaw rasped against her skin, and she moaned with the rough pleasure of it. Then he laved her belly, lower still, finding the agitated nub between her thighs. Sweetly, he licked the chocolate from the heated flesh, at first gentle, and then increasing the pressure. She jerked against the bonds, her hands frantic to touch, her body bucking with each wicked stroke of his tongue.

She could feel the climax building inside her, and her thighs locked over his shoulders, keeping him tight against her. His mouth increased, sucking almost painfully now, pulling her deeper and deeper into the vortex of passion that was going to—

Goddamn her. Sam pushed back from his computer, not believing what he was reading. Okay, she was mad at him, and he deserved it. But couldn't she have just called and yelled at him? Maybe written a nasty letter? Or dumped coffee on him? Any of those, including the hot coffee would be preferable to having his sexual performance laid out there for America to read in her blog.

Still, she hadn't used his name, and it wasn't close to what happened, but there was enough there to tick him off.

He picked up his car keys, ready to go into the city early. Right now, he had to go see a lady about a blog.

MERCEDES WAS ON HER seventh game of Solitaire when the buzzer rang. She pressed the intercom.

"It's Sam."

Sam? Mercedes buzzed him in, wishing she wasn't wearing the Juicy Couture sweats. Nothing said mature like having Juicy plastered on your butt. However, there wasn't time to change. She'd wing it, she always did.

When she opened the door, she took an immediate step back. It was Sam, all right. A new and different Sam. A mad Sam.

"What do you think you're doing?" he barked.

Okay, that wasn't the way it was supposed to be. "Why are you upset? If we have an upset party, then I'm the one who should be upset."

"Don't say that. What happened to us, just happened."

"Don't be such a hypocrite, Sam. It was planned. The CIA couldn't have executed with better precision."

His eyes lost a few degrees of their heat. The truth could do that. "Maybe so, but the reason I didn't pursue things any further was because of exactly what happened."

"What are you talking about?"

"Your blog."

Mercedes sighed, and began to pace, not caring a bit if Juicy was plastered on her butt. "Sam, I write a blog about sex. I've been doing this for almost two years now. I even talked about it on your show. Hello?"

"The last entry, Mercedes."

She met his eyes, locked her jaw. He wanted a fight about this? She was more than willing. "What about it?"

"Placid green eyes. Brown hair touched with gold. He thought he was too old for her."

Oh, God. She licked her lips, and her imagination leapt to her defense, just as it always did. "I write that character all the time, Sam. It's my old boyfriend. And besides, your eyes aren't green, they're hazel."

"You said they were green."

She took a step toward him, her features carefully composed. "You said they were hazel."

"You had an old boyfriend that looked like me?"

"Actually, I think 'you look like him' is the correct way to phrase it. Do you want to see a picture?"

He didn't look nearly as cocky. "The shoes, the stockings? Care to explain that?"

"Was there a bath in that story, Sam? Did water figure into it in any way?"

"No."

"A hotel room?"

"No."

"Was there chocolate in your hotel room, did you tie me up?"

"No," he said, his body alarmingly still.

"See. Of course it's not us." Oh, God. She'd written about him. Her mind didn't use details, just hazy figments of ideas. They weren't supposed to be real people, just creations.

He crossed his arms across his chest, his face still set

in stubborn lines. "I don't know why you did it. Maybe it was an accident, maybe you thought it'd be funny, or maybe you had planned to write something all along."

Mercedes jammed a finger against his chest. "Planned! You think I wrote about you on purpose? I've been accused of a lot of bad things, and most of them are true, but not this time."

"What am I supposed to think? Oh, hell, the why's don't matter. Find somebody else to write about, Mercedes."

"Don't flatter yourself."

"I told you my private life stays private. I knew it'd be a mistake."

After he left, Mercedes fell into a chair. The realization smacked her in the face. All these months. She'd been writing about *him*.

7

MERCEDES SPENT THE NEXT two days writing all sorts of steamy fantasies that involved black-haired men, red-haired men, but absolutely no brown-haired men at all. She even dreamed up a guy with a shaved head, just in case Sam was reading.

Green eyes were taboo. She used blue eyes, black eyes, and one with a pirate patch. But no green eyes—or hazel eyes, alternatively—were allowed.

She'd been silly not to see it, but her imagination wasn't like a high-definition television screen. It was fuzzy, a Vaseline-covered lens that was more like a dream.

Sam had thought she'd written about him on purpose, milking his fame for her own purposes. But it just happened, because Sam filled her head, crowding out all the normal made-up characters that lurked there, and that was what bugged her most of all.

When it came to men, Mercedes didn't have a brilliant track-record. Hell, it wasn't even a poor track-record and it traced all the way back to her father. A man she'd never known. A man who stuck around when Andrew and Jeff were kids, but had elected to bolt when Mercedes was born.

Her mother had said he wasn't a good man, his

eyes always searching for some new horizon. However, Mercedes wasn't sure. It always seemed to her that Mercedes was the problem. When you were a kid, it wasn't hard to make that leap, and after you got older, the rational brain explained it away, but the kid's brain still made that leap that somehow you were the reason he was gone. After all, he'd stuck around for Andrew and Jeff, but when Mercedes had been born—boom, out the door, don't forget to turn out the lights.

Just like all the men she dated.

But she suspected that Sam was different. Deep inside, hidden away from the world, hidden away from her mind, she *knew* he was different. He was a good man, he was a man that stayed around, and she didn't date that sort of a man—the kind you could fall for. She didn't want to fall for him, but that didn't stop her from writing in her blog, knowing that he was reading her words. It didn't stop her from wanting him to call.

Distractions came on Thursday, the appointed day for bridesmaid dress-shopping with Jamie, AKA Bridezilla Takes Manhattan.

The Bridal Stop was the go-to spot for all things wedding, although the store was enough to turn anyone off the institution of marriage. The displays were accented with baby's breath and pearls, and cute ring-bearer pillows. Dresses covered the walls, in colors from pastels to pinks, lilacs to lavender, and the forty-seven shades of pale purple in between. Even the air was scented with Bridal Mist fragrance, that smell of excitement and smug accomplishment at having snared a man for the kill. Whoever said men were the hunters had never watched a bride planning her wedding.

Mercedes didn't like weddings. They made her nervous. People made promises they wouldn't keep, promises for forever, or eight and a half years, whichever came first. No, the whole wedding business gave her the willies, but not Jamie. Oh, no, Jamie was in her element, her PDA stylus pushed behind one ear, and the checklist of items in her hand.

"Mercedes, I've located three Vera Wangs in a dark maroon, which should go well with your coloring, I think. Sheldon, for you, I got a Lazaro in royal blue, but I had them bring in two other Alvina Valenta designs, in case the blue and maroon clashed."

Jamie looked up from her checklist, spied the sales associate and pointed. "Do you have those silver shoes, two inch heels, pointed toe, but a little wide across the arch? I need to see those in—" She turned to Mercedes. "Size?"

"Seven and a half," answered Mercedes.

"Sheldon?"

"Six."

"Got that?"

The sales girl, used to the various idiosyncrasies of new, possibly hormonally charged brides-to-be, merely nodded.

"So, we do the dresses today, and if we get the shoes out of the way as well, then we're almost eighty percent to completion. Way to go, ladies."

Sheldon picked at the row of tiaras, and sat one on her head. On anybody else it would have been over the top, on Sheldon, she looked like a princess. Mercedes sighed wistfully.

Sheldon frowned in the mirror. "I've been thinking."

"About what?" asked Jamie, plucking at the tiara, frowning, and putting it safely away.

"I have this project I've been working on."

"You're going to rent yourself out as a professional bridesmaid and spare others the indignity?"

Sheldon made a face. "Please. No, this is something serious."

"Serious sounds serious."

Sheldon looked around nervously. "I'm starting a foundation. Music for kids in the inner-city. All the politicians are proposing to cut the funding for the arts, and I thought I could make a difference."

"Wow, that's so...so, worthy," said Mercedes.

"Do you think I can do it?"

"Hell, yeah, I think you can do it." Sheldon, being rich, and gorgeous, naturally had self-image problems. "Do you need help?" asked Mercedes.

"Yeah."

"I know absolutely nothing about fund-raising, nor am I musically gifted like you—"

"I'm not gifted."

"You play the violin. In my book, that's gifted."

"Fine. You'll help?"

"Yeah."

"Jamie?"

"I can spare four hours a week, six when it's not end of the quarter, but you'd be surprised what you can get done in a few hours."

"I'm always amazed," muttered Mercedes.

Right then, Jamie's PDA rang and she picked it up. "Hello?"

Her face turned dark.

"No, we're not having a horse-drawn carriage. A standard town-car is fine… That's what Andrew said?" Jamie asked, her face turning a shade darker. "Okay, let's table this until tomorrow. I'll give you a definitive answer then."

Jamie hung up and braced herself against the wall. "I've created a monster."

Mercedes tried not to smile, but it was difficult. Jamie didn't ever get flustered, but Mercedes had lived with Andrew during her formative years and she knew better. "Problem?"

Jamie blew out a breath. "Andrew. He keeps interfering in my wedding plans."

"Well, he is part of the ceremony," added Sheldon. "A key part."

"You don't understand. We had this discussion, almost a debate."

"An argument?" asked Mercedes.

"No, not an argument." Jamie worked her mouth for a moment, putting the words together. "In the beginning, we created a plan and a budget, and everything was wonderful. I was determined to stick to that plan, but then one of Andrew's golf buddies started bragging about his daughter's wedding, some big foofoo thing at St. Patrick's, and Andrew decided that I should have something bigger, more romantic. It's completely not like him to do this, but he's worried that I won't be satisfied. *I won't be satisfied?* He's going to blow our budget by four hundred percent. Now that will make me unsatisfied."

"He's made up his mind about this?" asked Mercedes,

because when Andrew made up his mind, well, it wasn't going to change. Jamie might as well throw in the towel now.

"I don't want doves or horse-drawn carriages," Jamie insisted.

"It could be worse," added Sheldon.

"How?"

"You could rent a Hummer Limo for the getaway car."

Mercedes laughed, because Jamie had met Andrew when they were forced to share a Hummer Limo ride to Connecticut. Complications ensued when they shared more than a ride.

However, instead of laughing, Jamie's eyes flashed with an a-ha gleam. "Sheldon, that's perfect!"

Sheldon looked startled. "Really?"

Jamie nodded, her lips curving up with fond memories. "Yes. But I want it to be a surprise. And no horse-drawn carriages. I will make this budget, I will."

Mercedes thought Jamie was fighting a losing battle, but Jamie was made of tough stuff. She sat down on the tiny, pearl-encrusted bench and looked at her sister-in-law-to-be. "Are you getting nervous?" she asked curiously.

"Why would I be nervous?"

Actually, Jamie seemed completely unfazed about putting her entire future into the hands of one man. "A lot of people would be nervous about getting married."

"Maybe so, but they aren't marrying Andrew."

Mercedes loved her brother, thought he was the best, but still….

"How're the book sales coming?" asked Sheldon.

Mercedes made a pickle face. "Eh."

Jamie looked up. "Your book's out?"

"Yes."

Jamie clicked into her PDA and then looked up triumphantly. "Just ordered seven copies from Amazon."

Mercedes's jaw dropped, awed at Jamie's super-caffeinated level of productivity. Mercedes was slightly in awe of her. "Thanks," Mercedes said. "It's appreciated."

"How was San Francisco? The show was pretty good. I TiVoed it, because GE was releasing their earnings after the market closed, and I needed to update a report for a client, but Andrew and I watched it later. I thought you were good."

The associate returned with the shoes, and Sheldon pulled hers on. "Your segment was too short, though, and Jeff said you kept tapping your fingers on the table. You really should let him give you media training. It'd help."

"Thanks," answered Mercedes, sitting in a chair, tugging off her shoes.

"How was Sam?" asked Sheldon, in a sly voice.

"Who?" asked Mercedes, trying not to remember his fingers on the arch of her foot.

"Your host?" asked Jamie, suddenly ganging up on her as well. At that point, Mercedes knew she'd been tag-teamed. Outmaneuvered by her brothers' wenches. It was demeaning, because at one time, nobody had pulled this off better than Mercedes herself. Pooh. She was slipping.

"Oh, that Sam. Yeah, he was good. Nice."

"What was the look for? The one you gave him right at the end of the show? Jeff said something that I can't repeat, but I was right there with him."

Mercedes forced a laugh. "I write sexy stuff, so I want to keep that image for the press. It's my persona."

Jamie stood, a shoe tapping in her hand. "Yeah, uh, huh."

Mercedes buried her face in her hands. "Guys, please don't tell me that I embarrassed myself on national TV."

Jamie came over and patted her on the shoulder. "I wouldn't have noticed it myself until Andrew pointed it out. He said you used to look at—what was that guy's name?"

"Johnny D'Amato?" offered Sheldon.

"Yup, that's the one. Andrew said you had it really, really bad for this Johnny dude in high school and you used to flash him the look. Did it work in high school?"

Mercedes lifted her head. "Yeah."

Sheldon wiggled her brows. "Did it work in San Francisco?"

"I am not saying a word. My lips are sealed. Not saying a word."

"That's a yes," laughed Jamie.

"It's a no."

Sheldon shook her head. "No, if it was a no, you would have just said no."

"It was a no," insisted Mercedes.

"Sure thing, Mercedes. We believe you."

"Can we try on dresses now?" asked Mercedes, needing to run away and hide in the dressing room before the evil women pulled more secrets out of her. She grabbed the fluted gown from the hanger, and zoomed into the dressing area.

"How's Andreas?" asked Sheldon.

Mercedes shrugged into the dress, pulling up the sleeves. "I broke up with him. Not that we were actually in a relationship that could be broken up, but in case he thought that, I broke up with him."

"Really? Why'd you do that?"

"Just tired of the B.S."

Sheldon giggled. "Mercedes? Mercedes Brooks? Is it the real Mercedes Brooks? You live and die by the B.S."

"Maybe in the past."

"There's a difference in the Mercedes of the past and the Mercedes of the now? Why?"

"I don't know," answered Mercedes, looking at herself in the mirror, and frowning. That was her, but it didn't feel like her. She felt older, smarter, sadder.

"I'm glad you broke up with him. He treated you like garbage and it's about time you realized it."

"He didn't treat me that bad."

"Did, too," added Jamie.

"Fine, judge me, all of you who are both happily involved in stable, healthy relationships."

"There's a guy at the office I could fix you up with," yelled Jamie. "He's nice, but he's a bit boring."

"No," answered Mercedes.

"What kind of guy do you want?" asked Sheldon.

"I don't know," replied Mercedes.

"Don't give me that. You write erotic fiction for a living. You have to know in explicit detail exactly what sort of man you want."

"Sex and a relationship are two different things," she explained patiently. "Sex is easy. Relationships are root canal-esque in their pain."

"Let's analyze the painful choice first, shall we? What do you want in a relationship?"

"He's got to be ripped," commented Jamie.

"Andrew isn't ripped," answered Mercedes, wondering if this tell-tale clue meant that the guy you fantasized about wasn't meant to be the guy you were meant to be with.

Jamie merely laughed.

"I don't want to think about my brother that way," said Mercedes.

Sheldon sighed. "Come on, Mercedes. What do you really want in a guy? I refuse to believe those pretty-boys are it."

"What's wrong with pretty-boys?"

"Mercedes, you are not answering the question."

"I know," said Mercedes.

"You don't know, do you?"

"I do," she protested, because it would be a weak-willed, yellow-bellied female who didn't know what she wanted in a relationship.

"What?" asked Jamie, completely unfooled.

Finally she thought of something. "I want a man who's reliable. Who won't stand me up, and won't ever leave me."

"Well, duh," answered Sheldon.

"And he's got to be funny. A sense of humor is very important. I want someone who can make me laugh. And he has to like food."

"What man doesn't like food?" asked Jamie.

"I dated this one guy who had some very weird eating habits," Sheldon mentioned. "He ate like a rabbit. Carrots and lettuce, and he'd wash them in a special rinse. It was too strange."

"Why did you date him?"

"I don't remember," Sheldon said. "But, I'm already

married, so let's talk about Mercedes. Her guy has got to be reliable, funny and like food. What color hair?"

Mercedes slipped the dress over her head. "I'm not inclined to judge someone on the basis of hair color," she told them, dodging this answer.

"What color hair?"

"Bald is very sexy," muttered Mercedes.

"Eyes?"

"Gray," snapped Mercedes.

"Icy. Nice."

"Okay, so we're looking for a balding, gray-eyed guy, late twenties, single, reliable, funny and must like food. That's it, Mercedes. He doesn't exist."

"I know he doesn't exist," agreed Mercedes. "Tell me something I don't know." Then she came out from the dressing room and twirled. "What do you think? It's your wedding. I'm merely the party favor."

Jamie looked her up and down, eyes taking in every minute detail. "It looks good. Sheldon?"

Sheldon appeared as a chic concoction that made her look more gorgeous than usual. Mercedes exhaled, at least as far as her dress would allow. "Do I have to stand next to her? I look like the ugly step-sister beside her.

Sheldon caught Mercedes in a one-armed hug. "You're not my step-sister."

"Very funny."

"Oh, come on. Be a sport. You look gorgeous."

"Not as gorgeous as you."

Jamie looked at them both critically. "No. But I like it."

"This is it? No more dress fittings?"

"Unless you want more—" started Jamie.

"No!" said Sheldon and Mercedes together.

"Ah, consensus. Ladies, we have a wedding wardrobe portfolio." She called over the associate. "We'll take these."

"I think it's time to celebrate. Something with chocolate."

Mercedes picked at the tight fabric at her waist, checking for excess room. "Can we skip the chocolate? If I'm supposed to look good in this dress, I have to lose five pounds."

Sheldon grinned in the evil manner of a woman who had never dieted in her life. "Starting tomorrow."

Mercedes laughed again, wondering how good chocolate worked on loneliness because the bubble baths weren't cutting in anymore.

THERE WAS NOTHING LIKE A woman to confuse a man. Since Sam had fought with Mercedes, he'd read her blog religiously, looking for any hint, any mention, any clue that might represent him. None were to be found.

Now, he was getting pissed off, because she was writing about sexual relations with pretty-boys with flowing black locks that fell in their eyes, and poet-like dimples in their chin. What was that all about? And the posts were coming fast and furious. Ten and eleven times a day the entire weekend. He wanted to believe this was pure fiction, he knew it was pure fiction. But ten or eleven times a day, four days in a row? Man, that put some serious pressure on a guy.

Sam checked his watch and realized he had a meeting with the writers in less than half an hour. He couldn't sit here in his studio office reading her blog. He minimized her site, then pulled out the first draft of tonight's script. He'd barely gotten to page three when Charlie came in his office.

"My friend called back," he said, settling into the chair across from Sam.

"What friend?"

"I told you about him. Harvey. Party Chairman. New Jersey. Election. Campaign. Remember?"

"You mentioned him, but you neglected to mention he was a friend," said Sam, arching a brow. "You called him my fan. I remember."

Charlie squinted up at the lights. "Friend. Fan. We play golf together on Sundays."

"That's another fact you neglected to mention, Charlie. I like knowing all the facts. Any other facts that might be missing here?"

"Well, hell, Sam, I thought you'd jump at the chance to get into the thick of things, and I'd explain it to you slowly, parcel it out a bit at a time, so you'd figure you came up with this all on your own. So, have you come to any conclusions?" Charlie finished his speech, looking at Sam expectantly.

"I've been thinking…"

"Yeah?" drawled Charlie.

Sam gave him a nod. "Yeah. Let me talk to this guy."

"I knew you'd say that. Meet us over at the Four Seasons Sunday night."

"This was already set up?"

"Two days ago. You had a restless look in your eye. Figured you were coming round."

Sam wasn't about to explain the cause of the restless look to Charlie, better to let him think that politics was the cause of his problems. In truth, he was more interested in pursuing the candidacy than he realized. "You were right. When you're right, you're right."

Charlie smiled. "Martin Darcy is going to be there, too. He's the best campaign manager on the Atlantic seaboard. Got a dark-horse candidate elected in the West Virginia Senate, and swung a huge upset in California in the 2000 elections. He's our man, Sam. If we're going to do this, we're going to do it right."

"And here I thought I was the cash cow."

"Aw, Sam. I'm going to turn seventy-two next year. I'm too old to have cash cows. Now's the time when I get to be a god-maker, play with history." He pointed a stubby finger at Sam. "Now there's where a man makes his mark, not with cash, or television."

"I knew you were connected, Charlie, but I never knew how much."

Charlie smiled. "Politics are best left behind closed doors, know what I mean?"

"Unless you make a career out of talking about them."

"That's you, not me."

After Charlie left, Sam went back to the script, making changes and adding notes as he read. When he finished the script, he turned to the computer.

And voila. Another entry. Somebody had been busy.

The pain was becoming harder to bear. The suspicious glances, the questions in his voice, as if he didn't trust me. What hurt most was that I had done things, but never what he'd accused me of. Each night we slept together, almost strangers in our lovemaking, together, yet alone, and I couldn't bear it any more. A rubber band pulled tightly will have no choice but

to break. It took me two weeks to gather my courage
to buy the poison, but eventually I had it in my hands.
He came home, and I poured his usual diet soda, un-
wrapping the tiny packet from the cabinet. I hesitated, shaking fingers trying to decide….

Poison?

Just then, Kristin burst in. "Sam, here's the bio on the
Connecticut mayor who wanted to outlaw Thanksgiv-
ing." Her eyes looked at the monitor behind him. "Red
Choo Diaries. Is that…?" Then she looked at him and
laughed. "What the heck are you doing?"

"Research," he said, using his thoughtful, professor
look.

"Sure, Sam. You be careful before the IT security
goons have you written up for viewing unsuitable ma-
terials at work. It doesn't matter that you're the star. To
security, you're just another faceless userid."

Sam held out his hand for the paper. "I'll take that
under advisement. Let me read the bio and get back to
you on whether we want him on the show or not."

"Okay, boss. Isn't that the Brooks woman's site?"

"Goodbye, Kristin."

"Goodbye, Sam. But remember what I said. Don't
get caught," and then she slammed the door behind her.

Sam reread the part about the poison, looked at his soda
and sniffed. No bitter almond smell there. He was safe.

Maybe he had been too hard on her. He'd seen the
shell-shocked look in her face when he'd accused her
of writing about them on purpose. So she had some fantasies about him, how could a man be mad about that?

On the other hand, she'd put them out there, opened

up his bedroom door for all of America to read. Sam hated the idea of people reading about something so intensely personal, even if it was anonymous. He needed his space from the world of television. Unlike Mercedes, Sam didn't want the public prying into his private life.

Although if anything came out, it could be explained away as an inside joke. She'd been on his show. She thought it'd be funny to write him that way. It almost sounded plausible when he stuck to the facts as the world needed to know them.

Almost.

8

SAM ARRIVED HOME THAT evening and sent Max outside for his nightly business. Sam hadn't planned on clicking back to her blog, however, the lure of the Net called, and he was curious to see if Mercedes had posted anything more.

There were two new stories, raising her daily quota to nine. One was a dark S&M piece, with lots of leather, some rope, and nipple rings, all of which made him wary. Did she like bondage? Was she out there somewhere right now, sheathed in leather and chains, tied, being pleasured until…

No. Man, he didn't get into bondage, but his Johnson must've missed the memo. It only took a split-second mental visual of that tight body in leather, and Sam was wondering if he'd been missing out on something. Max looked up and barked.

"Yeah. I know. Stick to the sports car."

Thankfully, her second piece was more suitable for a man of his years and political persuasion. A couple that was locked in a sauna. Steamy, literally.

There were no more poisons, no guns, and no anger. Things were improving. Which left Sam with something of a choice.

Mercedes was a woman who wrote erotic fiction that included leather, chains and nipple rings. Sam spent his Sunday's going to the early mass and watching football, maybe getting crazy and splurging with a second beer.

He was thirty-nine, seriously considering a run for Congress.

She was twenty-six, intent on writing, blogging and titillating her way to fame and fortune.

Those were the facts.

It wasn't pretty. What it was was a statistical improbability. However, that didn't change the one fact that he couldn't stop thinking about her—nipple rings and all.

And he was thirty-nine, not seventy-nine. Up to now his life had been set on a cruise-control ride to the top. Ten years ago he had worked his tail off, but now he felt more comfortable phoning it in. He had settled into a routine that suited him.

Mercedes shook him out of the complacency. He wouldn't be thinking twice about a Congressional run if he hadn't been able to imagine her face lighting up at the thought. And instead of hitting the hay at midnight, he'd been staying up late, haunted by thoughts of one night in San Francisco. He replayed it, cut and spliced the tape inside his head.

They'd spent less than forty-eight hours together, but with Mercedes, after ten minutes, you knew her deep down to her heart. He'd seen her heart—among other parts—and he liked her heart.

And that was it. Decision made.

Sam picked up the phone to call her, apologize, make things right. He got the sultry voice of her answering machine and hung up. He never left messages if it was a personal call because he hated voice mail. Another artificial barrier to separate humanity even further.

He stared at the phone, wondering if she was screening her calls, or was she actually out in leather and spiked heels, one hand on the whip at her side? Both scenarios bothered him, although one strangely aroused him as well. Sam let in Max, and got himself a beer from the refrigerator.

The news played in the background, and he read some of the pieces on the New Jersey political environment that Charlie had given him. After he finished, he looked at the clock, looked at wide-awake Max.

Where was she?

Idly he picked up the Daily News, and reread the article that had caught his attention earlier. He dug through his computer e-mails and came across the source he was looking for. The more info he had on one Mercedes Brooks, the better.

SHELDON BROOKS DIDN'T usually watch television at night, but then again, her husband wasn't usually glued to his computer. Technically they were still in the honeymoon phase, and if he was going to be glued to anything at night, it'd be her.

She sighed, arching languidly in bed, trying to distract him. He looked up, ogling her for a minute, and then shook a warning finger. "Thirty more minutes. Swear."

"You said that," she looked at the clock, "twenty-seven minutes ago."

She tilted one shoulder, letting the strap of her teddy slip lower. Jeff's dark gaze grew even more distracted.

"I could take a break," he offered in the spirit of maintaining marital harmony.

She gave him her sultriest smile. This was the man she knew and loved. "Take me, I'm yours."

He pounced, and was settling in on the special spot behind her ear when the phone rang.

Sheldon was prepared to let the answering machine pick up, because she really liked that special spot, but then she heard the voice on their machine.

She put a hush-finger to her lips and picked up.

"Hello," she said, sending Jeff an apologetic glance. She'd have things to make up for later, but that wasn't a problem.

"Sheldon Brooks? Sam Porter here. I'm sorry to call so late."

"Oh, it's not too late," she said, talking while trying to keep Jeff's talented hands and mouth at bay.

"Your sister-in-law mentioned something last week about a new charity project, and I was curious if you'd like to come on the show, to help out a good cause, of course."

"That's very nice of you."

"I believe in philanthropy, people helping people."

"I'm sure we could arrange something. Why don't you have your booker talk to Tower Communications, and arrange the time and place. It was great of you to think of me. I know you're a busy man, so I'll just—"

"Wait!"

"Yes," asked Sheldon, trying desperately not to laugh. After all, this was Mercedes's love life, and she shouldn't find anything remotely humorous about it. But after what Mercedes had put her through with that blog, there was a certain satisfaction in payback.

"About Mercedes. Is she doing okay?"

"Mercedes? You know, now that you mention it, she was pretty depressed the other day. A shadow of the woman she usually was. You know where she is right now? Home alone, watching the soap opera channel, and she hates soap operas. I don't think she's eating, either."

Jeff looked up, alarmed, and she shook her head.

"She's really feeling bad?" He sounded fabulously concerned, and Sheldon sighed heavily into the phone.

"Awful. I wish I knew what was wrong. You don't know, do you?"

He hesitated, a tell-tale sign that no woman over the age of puberty would miss. "No, not a clue."

"It could be the book, I suppose."

"What's wrong with the book?"

"I shouldn't say anything, but she's worried about her sales numbers."

"You think that's what's bothering her?"

"I don't think so. I think this is more serious than that. So why were you asking about Mercedes?"

He paused again, and Sheldon could tell that deception didn't come easy to Sam. He'd have much to learn to survive in this family. Finally he spoke. "She was supposed to contact me about something, and I haven't heard from her."

"You should try and call her."

"That's a good idea. I think I will. Book sales, huh?"

"Yeah."

"Thanks for your help."

"Anytime."

Sheldon hung up and burst out laughing.

"What was that about?" asked Jeff. "What's wrong with Mercedes?"

"Nothing that can't be fixed by one Mr. Sam Porter."

"That was Sam Porter?" He started to laugh, too. "You're a devious woman, Mrs. Brooks."

"Why thank you, Mr. Brooks. Now come and do your husbandly duty."

He kissed her, and she happily kissed him back, forgetting about everyone's love life but her own.

THE NEXT MORNING, SAM tried to call Mercedes again, but she wasn't answering at her apartment, or on her cell, and he still refused to leave a message. At lunchtime he headed for the studio, making a stop at the bookstore on Route 17. Her display was up there near the front, and Sam decided the picture didn't do her justice. Three dimensions were necessary to capture the full effect of Mercedes Brooks.

She had that way, that vibrancy about her. She dared a man to come out and play. To do more, to be more. He picked up a copy of her book and walked toward the registers. If she wanted to be a success, he would do his part.

By buying another book? One, single book? What sort of crappy dent would that make?

He loaded up all the copies on the display and took them to the front.

"You're getting all these?" asked the clerk.

"Yeah," Sam stated, praying the clerk wouldn't recognize him while he was buying an armload of erotica. It wouldn't do much for his family-friendly image.

The clerk picked up the credit card, glanced at his name. "Can I see some ID, sir?"

Sam fished out his wallet, expecting the recognition

any minute, and preparing himself for the first amendment constitutional response. Casual insolence, protector of free speech, and a man who believed that all reading material was created equal. "Sure," he said, handing over his license.

The clerk held it up and compared his signature to the signature on the credit card. "Sorry, sir. I can't take this."

"Excuse me?"

"It looks fake."

"It's not fake," Sam managed through clenched teeth.

"It looks fake. It's a good copy, but the watermark isn't there."

Sam pointed to his driver's license. "It's there."

"I'm sorry, sir."

The manager came forward, sensing a crisis, and smiled politely. "May I help you, sir?"

"His credit card is bogus," said the kid.

"It's not bogus," argued Sam.

"And the driver's license is a fake."

The manager looked at Sam. "You're Sam Porter?"

Sam nodded once.

The manager looked at the kid. "This is real."

"No way. That credit card was fake, you could tell by the way the little plastic numbers—"

"Can you just ring it up?" asked Sam.

The manager glanced at the pile of Mercedes's books. "You're buying these?"

Casually Sam leaned against the mahogany counter like he did this every day. If he wanted a relationship with Mercedes, this was what he was in for. He could do this. He locked his face in a smile. "Uh-huh. If you have any more in the back, I'll take those as well."

The manager blinked, but then lifted the phone. "Give me a second."

"I'll wait," answered Sam, trying to blend into the crowd. But people had started to gawk, and it wasn't easy. One man was eyeing the cover of Mercedes's book and Sam slowly flipped the top copy over—because all reading material wasn't created equal, no matter what the librarians said.

Eventually the manager returned with another three books. "Should I add these to your purchase?"

"Go ahead," said Sam.

"You're certainly getting a lot of these," murmured the manager as the kid rang up the additional purchases.

"It's for a friend." Okay, so maybe he wasn't quite ready for America to know what Sam Porter was reading late at night.

"Uh-hum," said the manager, skepticism oozing through every priggy pore in his body.

"It's a joke I'm playing on someone," lied Sam, angry that a man couldn't buy seventeen copies of an erotic novel without feeling embarrassed enough to lie about it. He should be brave. He should tell the truth, explain he was doing this to help out a friend. It was a good deed; there was absolutely no reason in the world to feel defensive about it.

"Ah," replied the manager, finally finding an explanation he could buy into.

Sam didn't disabuse him. So he wasn't that brave of a man. Big deal. He had other qualities.

He kept hitting bookstores, until he had bought up almost two hundred copies of *The Red Choo Diaries,* his trunk and backseat full of the sexual writings of one

Mercedes Brooks. Why couldn't she have written a normal book? *Hunting for Dummies, Real Men Eat Steak.*

Somehow he knew that Mercedes would never be normal. Ever. He laughed to himself. Normal or not, he still wanted her. Maybe she was the psychological equivalent of a sports car, maybe not. It didn't change things. Her stories didn't change things, leather skirts didn't change things, a campaign for Congress wouldn't change things, either.

No matter how complicated, Sam still wanted her.

Bad.

IT TOOK ONE MORE DAY TO break him. On Saturday afternoon, he left a message on her answering machine. "It's Sam. I hope you're home and not tied up somewhere. I'm sorry."

Five days. The man had more backbone than a humpback whale. She'd written five days worth of literary murder, mayhem, even delving into whips and chains, which normally weren't her thing. Fiction wasn't life, and she hoped Sam got the point, and so what if he got a little nervous—whatever.

It still ticked her off when she thought about it. Mercedes wasn't some groupie, using him to get rich quick. *That* had opened up an artery that she didn't know she had.

The sharp pain inside her was why she didn't like relationships, why she danced her way in and out of affairs with jerky men. But Sam wasn't jerky, and somewhere in her head, "just one night" had changed into "just another night."

Part of her problem was the wiggling worm of guilt that ate inside her. In the past she had cavalierly used her writing for her own purposes, and if other people were involved, it'd taken a back seat to her achieving her dreams. She had inched very, very close to hurting Andrew and Jeff by writing anonymous entries about their private lives in her blog that were more fact than fiction—with a dash of creative license thrown in. She'd tried to be careful and skirt the line, but careful wasn't the same as not writing it at all. No, she'd done it, because Mercedes had a dream of being a successful writer.

This time, when it was Sam—and her, the light bulb inside her began to glow. This time, she got it. Dreams were a good thing, but not at the cost of the people you cared about.

His short, simple phone message went a long way to ease the hurt, ease the guilt, and move their "not really a relationship" into something else. In only thirteen words, she knew that he trusted her. Very few people trusted Mercedes, even her brothers were nervous, but Sam….

Sam did.

It was from a happier place that she began to work on her blog. This time, she wasn't so cruel, because she owed him an apology too. Sam liked his privacy, she knew that.

The message on her answer machine had been exactly what she wanted to hear. She loved his voice, loved the way he lingered over her name. He had been overseas, but would be coming home soon, home to her. She climbed into bed, missing the warm spot that belonged to him. The television helped, but it didn't make up for the strength of his body, the way he held her in his arms.

Soon. Very, very soon…

Sam smiled at the words. Things were definitely improving. He called, got her answering machine and decided he would destroy that wretched piece of technology as soon as he got the chance.

As much as he'd rather spend a crisp Sunday afternoon with Mercedes, he had a life-altering meeting to think about. He wanted to treat this one like any other meeting he attended, but there was a humming in his gut that said otherwise.

Today he was meeting Charlie and his two cohorts at Ben Benson's. Ben Benson's—now that was a place for men. The chairs were black, the meat was red, and the beer ran icy cold. Restaurants didn't get much better than that.

A wreck on the Palisades made him later than expected, and when he got there the other men were already seated, nursing their drinks.

Martin Darcy was very smooth, from his moussed hair to his polished leather uppers. His smile was perfect, his teeth were capped, and Sam suspected he lived and died by his poll numbers.

"Sam Porter. Whew. What a shining star for the party. I saw the piece you did on California's influence on the Supreme Court. Poetry, sir. Pure poetry."

Sam nodded graciously. "Thank you."

Harvey tapped his fingers restlessly on the table. He had the leathered-old skin of a blue-collar man, and yet he was the party chairman. "But we're not here to talk about poetry."

Martin picked up the hint. "No, we're here to get you signed on for the primaries. Our opposition is closing around Tommy Ferguson for their candidate and he's good. Squeaky clean, but a big zero on the charisma-meter. I think we play up your Jimmy Stewart/Clint Eastwood qualities, and that way we'll woo the soccer moms and the NRA, all at the same time." He pulled out some papers. "I've got a platform laid out for you—"

Sam pushed the papers back. "Shouldn't I have some input here?"

Harvey coughed. "Martin's only giving you a jumping off point. Part of the reason you're admired is that you're not lock-step in with everyone else, and we're going to use that, not change it. You run a little more centrist than some of the right-wingers want, but you'll charm them."

Sam looked over the documents. "I'll read these and see what I like."

"Very good," Martin said with a landslide in November smile. "Did you ever do a piece on the campaign trail? Follow anyone around?"

"Back in the early nineties. The local news sent me on the bus with the gubernatorial candidate. I've had candidates on the show, but I've only been in front of the camera."

Martin snorted. "Not a problem. You're quick. You won't believe some of the jackasses I've had to work with."

"Doesn't matter as long as you can get those jackasses elected," Sam said smoothly.

Charlie laughed. "You'll have to go easy on Sam, Martin. He's a little set in his ways."

Sam folded his arms across his chest, not bothering to disagree.

Martin looked at Sam, looking at Harvey, and then nodded. "Any skeletons, on-the-air quotes, or flag-burnings we should know about?"

"Nothing but a few parking tickets."

"Wife?"

"Divorced for over ten years. I'm assuming that dating a porn star, an erotica writer, or a flag-burning liberal would be out of the question?"

Martin stabbed a finger in the air. "You're going to be great on the stump, I can see it now."

Sam coughed. "There's nothing to worry about, but my private life is nobody's but mine."

"As long as it's clean," said Martin, who then lifted his drink. "To the next Congressman from the great state of New Jersey."

Glasses were clinked, backs were patted, and Sam smiled blandly.

Hell.

9

THE NEXT MORNING, SAM showed up at her door, unannounced, uninvited, and there was no one she wanted to see more.

"We're speaking now?" she asked cautiously, letting him in. His eyes looked tired, and his usually tousled hair was a little more tousled than usual. She kept her eyes guarded as her gaze slipped over him. This wasn't usual for her, either. Usually she didn't care.

"Speaking, yes. I think that's what they call this." His hazel eyes gentled to the green of the spring grass. She wanted to stand there, sinking deeply into their tenderness. "I'm sorry I said what I said. I know you didn't do it on purpose, Mercedes."

"I'm sorry I did what I did. I didn't realize, then. I do now."

He held out his hand and she laid hers over it, such a small touch, such a big step for her. In the past, an argument meant walking out the door without flinching. This time, she flinched. This time she stayed.

Sam had no idea what this cost her, and she was determined to keep that hidden. After all, two television shows, one dinner, and one endless night, did not a relationship make. Mercedes shook her hair carelessly, like this was no big deal, and this time, Sam flinched, too.

The heat from the eyes cooled—not a lot, but she noticed. He checked his watch.

"Hey, what are you doing now? I've got seventy-five minutes to kill until I have to be in the studio, and I need to get a birthday present for my sister-in-law. I'm really bad at presents."

"You're really bad at presents?"

"The worst."

Wow, an actual character deficiency. Mercedes was charmed. "You're very lucky that I'm an expert shopper. Where are we going?"

"You're in charge."

Mercedes picked up her long leather coat and grabbed her bag from the hook by the door. "Macy's. It's the shopping mecca. If you can't get something there, you're a lost cause."

"Nice coat," he said, his eyes skimming over her. "You like leather, huh?"

"Doesn't everybody?"

"It's growing on me."

They walked out of her building into the brisk fall air. To the east, the river, to the west, the booming Manhattan skyline, and above it all, the sun maintained order, high in the sky. Fluffy clouds drifted by slowly. It was perfect.

"Cab or walk?" he asked.

She glanced at him, glanced at the sky. "Walk."

He gave her a nod and they were off. His strides were long, but growing up with two older brothers, Mercedes was used to walking fast and keeping up.

"Tell me about your sister-in-law. What would she like?" she asked, starting to reach for his hand. But then a man passed by on the street, looking at Sam once, looking at Sam twice. Sam Porter. Mercedes stuffed her hands in her pockets.

He didn't even notice the looks. "I don't know. That's why you're here."

"Does she like clothes, cooking, candy or knick-knacks?"

"Yes, no, she's diabetic, and maybe. The house is covered with the little horrors."

"What did you get her last year?"

"I'm supposed to remember? Let me think… A gift certificate…I think."

Mercedes groaned.

"Hey, she liked it," he said defensively.

Such a babe in the woods. Mercedes would have to educate him. "That's what she told you. People don't tell you to your face that they hate the gift." She looked at him, shook her head. "A gift certificate?"

"It's a very practical gift, and it was for a restaurant that my brother likes."

"You have much to learn, Sam."

"I'm putty in your hands."

She winked at him, then, and he smiled, and maybe they weren't holding hands, but he was touching her in ways that he didn't realize.

They walked on, across 14th, up Broadway, and there were more subtle looks in Sam's direction. No one stopped him, but people saw, and Mercedes took it all in. New Yorkers were very casual about celebrity, and the ratio of talk show hosts to average citizens was higher in Manhattan, than, for instance, Iowa. But the aura was still there, hanging over him.

Deliberately she kept her hands in her pockets and walked. Touching was overrated anyway.

They hit 34th Street, and she pulled him into Macy's and the shopping safari began in earnest. Her first destination was the top floor where the china department was located. Sam examined the dinner plates and goblets, then examined her. "She doesn't like to cook. I told you. This is cooking."

"Not cooking. That's in the basement. This is tableware." Mercedes led him over to the glassware and picked a piece up. "And we call this a crystal vase. We add some silk flowers, then pick out a nice little pin, and top it off with a gift certificate from her favorite restaurant."

"I thought gift certificates were bad."

"You can accessorize with a gift certificate, but it cannot be the primary."

"Says who?" he asked, in his skeptical, interviewing voice.

"The Rules," answered Mercedes patiently. She'd been on the receiving end of skepticism many times, and had learned to bulldoze right through it.

"What rules? It's a present."

"There are gifting rules. Follow and learn. First we need to establish her favorite restaurant."

"What if I don't know Linda's favorite restaurant?"

"You ask your brother."

Next they headed for the jewelry section, where Mercedes picked through the costume jewelry until at last she lifted a pin to the light. "Perfect."

Sam stared. "What is it?"

"It's a shoe."

"A shoe? Are you sure she'll like a shoe?"

"Yes, she'll like a shoe *pin*. It's compact, cute, yet tasteful enough to go with a variety of styles, both modern and classic."

Sam shook his head. "It just looks like a shoe to me, sorry."

"She'll love it," she said, and patted his hand. She meant the touch as a joke, but he caught her fingers for a second, and held them there. Her smile died, and then she pulled her hand away.

As they were walking by the men's department she accidentally guided him into the densely overgrown, subterranean polyester-cotton-cashmere jungle of men's shirts. Flannel was nice, but he should have something new, more up to date. After all, he had a public image to consider. He must have spied her predatory glance, because he pulled back, away from the jumble of racks and displays. "I like my shirts."

"It's plaid," she explained, which she thought was explanation enough.

Sam glanced down at his shirt. "There are no rules for shirts. Plaid is good."

"Plaid is bad. Although, if you went with a Scottish plaid in wool, it might be okay."

"I'm not dressing like some damned highlander, Mercedes."

"And the lumberjack look is okay?"

"You don't like my shirt?"

"I love your shirt. But I think it could be even better. You're a very handsome man, and in the right shirt…" she trailed off.

He looked away, his jaw locked in that no-argument position she was beginning to recognize. "No. I'm not buying a shirt."

"I could buy you a shirt," she offered.

"I don't need you to buy me a shirt."

Mercedes pulled him over to the nice *GQ*-dude who worked the department. "Tell him he needs a new shirt."

"I don't need a new shirt."

"Sir, you need a new shirt."

Mercedes smiled at the man. "Thank you. I tried to tell him. I'm his sister and it's very frustrating to get him to wear anything nice."

"She's not my sister. I'm not getting a shirt."

Mercedes picked up a black silk shirt, then looked him over.

"No."

"What size are you?" she asked.

"No," repeated Sam.

The suit looked him over. "Thirty-eight, I would guess." Sam glared at the suit, who smiled politely back.

"We'll take this in a thirty-eight."

"I don't want a black shirt, Mercedes."

"It'll look very good on you, sir. Pick up the highlights in your hair."

"I don't have highlights in my hair," said Sam.

"I love your highlights," said Mercedes. "I'm not really his sister. Actually a second-cousin. His mother married my uncle Frank's step-sister, Delia. That'd be second-cousins, wouldn't it? Don't you find family trees confusing?"

"Oh, for goodness sake. Let's just pay for the shirt and get out of here."

Mercedes beamed at him. And in less than fifteen minutes, they were out the door with Linda's present in hand.

"You need to go?" asked Mercedes, noticing when he glanced at his watch. She didn't like the catch in her voice, that needy, "don't leave me" quiver.

The subway rumbled beneath them, and Sam pulled the phone from his pocket. With a one-thumbed flick, he powered it off. "What's a few minutes?"

Mercedes felt an extra kick in her heart, and her lips curved upwards, completely needy, but she was too happy to care.

"I need caffeine," she said, so he bought her a cup of coffee and they walked up 6th Avenue to Bryant Park. The fall crowds were quieter than in summer, but the chess players still came out, bundled in their sweaters and hats, and the pond had just opened the ice, and was teeming with afternoon skaters.

They found two chairs near the edge of the lawn and sat, watching the skaters. Mercedes pushed back the hair from her face, trying to be casual, but she could feel him watching her.

"You shop well."

"I practice often. You're fun to shop with. We should do it again."

"Not anytime soon," he said. "You have plans for next Friday?"

"No plans except for laundry."

He glared.

"But I can do that on Saturday," she offered.

"I have a friend who's going through a divorce and he needs cheering up. Get back in the swing of things.

I thought we could go to a club, maybe let him work up to an actual date."

"A club? That's very indiscreet of you."

"We'll be okay. It's not my target market. You're more likely to be recognized than me, and we'll have Tony there, too."

"Tony?"

"Tony, that's the divorced one. He needs to get out some."

"Have you set him up with a profile on the Web?"

"What?"

"A dating profile. He should do that, let the women come to him, and he can sort through them."

"You think he should?"

Mercedes nodded. "It'll be perfect. I'll help with his profile and soon the women will be flocking to him in droves."

"But you don't even know him."

"Well, he's a friend of yours. Why shouldn't I help?"

"I'll talk to him."

"Do you think I should bring a friend on Friday? Make this a group outing? Good buddies, doing favors in the name of absolutely nothing remotely sinful and wicked."

"I'll let you decide. Either we go out and you help him with the meeting strange women part, or else you bring a friend that won't savage his ego."

"Fragile?"

He nodded.

She considered the options. "Let's wing this. I think he's better off dealing with a whole roomful of women than one who might expect things from him.

Besides, if anyone notices, that way nobody will know who I'm with."

He frowned at her. "No. You'll be with me."

"I know that, but they won't know that, and we don't have to let them know that."

He reached out, took a strand of hair between his fingers. Tempting fate, she supposed. "It's very hard not to touch you," he said, his voice husky and rough.

Mercedes leaned in closer, not touching, but close enough to feel the warmth emanating from him. She let her eyes linger on his face, as real as any caress.

"I thought this was easier for you. To the world you always seem so controlled."

He laughed. "Right."

"Tell me what you'd do."

He glanced at her, his eyes hard, but she saw the images there. Him. Her. Together. "One night isn't nearly enough, Mercedes. Every time I touch you, or see you, or even smell your perfume, I turn. It's like some Jekyll & Hyde condition. All I can think about is losing your clothes, seeing the moonlight on your skin, the long line of your thigh, your breasts in my hands, in my mouth. I want to touch you, taste you when you come."

Her breathing slowed to nothing, her breasts swollen as if his hands were there, her nipples hard, as if his mouth was there. At her center, her throbbing, aching center, she could feel the dampness between her thighs, as if his tongue was already there.

"You're a very dangerous man, Sam Porter. You're all easygoing and charming, with that casual smile, and then BOOM my underwear is drenched and I swear if we were alone I'd—"

He stopped her with a hand to her mouth. "Don't. I've got to interview a Harvard law professor in less than two hours, and I can't go in there with your voice echoing in my head."

Her tongue flicked against his palm, and he jerked it back, as if he'd been burned.

"I'm better with the head than the hand," she whispered.

Quietly he groaned. "I've never done this, been like this. Wound up like a top, spinning on nothing. In the past, all my relationships have been standard, ordinary, a few dates, sex. Everything was comfortable. I wish we could have ordinary, but right now that's impossible. I wish…ah, hell. Even if it wasn't comfortable, I wouldn't feel so bad."

"Why do you feel bad?"

"It doesn't bother me what you do; I'm learning to like it, even."

"But it might bother some people, right? Sam, you need to know something. I like what you do, too. I like the show, I like your idealism. The world needs that more than I need dinner at Nobu. I don't need dates and ordinary. There's a word. Discretion. I'm learning it."

"I don't like doing this in secret. This isn't Victorian England."

"Well, no, and thank God, because you'd have a fit if they put you in knickers."

"I want to touch in public, Mercedes. I want to walk down the street holding your hand."

"We can hold hands behind closed doors. And I can cook, you know. And there's a great new invention. DVDs. Perhaps you've heard of them? Oh, wait. I bet you get first-run stuff, don't you?"

"Only the G-rated ones. Sorry."

She sighed. "Okay, fine. So I get no privileges from your position. I can live with that. I want to live with that, Sam. We try, we see what happens. And you come over. I'll cook. Get a bottle of wine. We can watch the sunrise over the fire escape in the building across the street. It's very romantic."

"What are you doing tonight?"

"Cooking? Drinking wine? Watching the sun rise over the fire escape? It's been known to happen when the moon is in the right phase, and Jupiter aligns with Mars. Eight o'clock?"

"Probably closer to nine. We have some wrap-up work after the taping."

"You lead a hard life, Sam."

"I know. Take pity on me."

She pressed a quick kiss on his cheek. A mere peck. "I'll leave the whips and chains in the closet."

There was panic in his eyes, and she shrugged. Let him wonder. Besides, she was seeing him tonight. Everything else didn't matter.

THE CANDLES SHIMMERED IN the dimmed light, the wax pooling and dripping over the edges. Mercedes had cleaned, she had cooked, she had bathed, she had dressed. Everything was ready, except she had no date.

The ziti was turning from a beautiful, bubbling amber to a not-so-beautiful, burning brown and Mercedes pulled it out of the oven, fighting tears. Everything was supposed to be perfect.

She kept telling herself that if a man was thirty minutes late, it did not mean he would never show up at her door again. Sam was reliable. Not punctual, perhaps, but reliable. Sam was not going to disappear.

After spending a good five minutes cursing the whims of Harvard law professors, Italian pasta and a certain nameless man who had no concept of time, the phone rang.

It was said nameless man, who had miraculously developed the concept of time.

"Hey, I'm still at the studio. Got caught up in a problem with tomorrow's show. I'll be there, but it'll probably be another hour."

"No problem," muttered Mercedes.

"You're mad."

"No. You're a busy guy, and if I spent four hours slaving over a hot burner, and have to sit and watch all that hard work turn cold—"

"Eat without me."

"That's not the point."

"I'm sorry. I'll be out of here as soon as I can."

As soon as I can. Mercedes should have known better. At the end of the day, all men were unreliable creatures—including Sam, which ticked her off even more, because she had held him up to a higher standard, and he had failed the test.

She scowled into the phone. "That's okay, I'll take another bath."

"A bath?" he asked, his voice perking up.

"Yeah," she murmured, almost a purr.

"Bubbles?"

"You tell me."

"No bubbles. You like your baths, don't you?"

"You catch on quick."

"I could help," he offered.

"But you have to work," she said sadly.

"I'm not feeling well. Fever. Very bad. Must go soon."

Mercedes kicked off her heels.

"What was that?" he asked, not sounding remotely ill.

"My shoes."

"I'll be there in seven minutes."

10

THE CANDLES WERE NOTHING but tiny stubs, the ziti sat uneaten on the table, and the wine was still unopened. Towels were strewn like bread crumbs from the bath to the couch, where Mercedes was curled up next to Sam, all transgressions now easily forgiven. A few well-timed orgasms would do that to a girl.

He tightened his arms around her. "Next time I think you need to come to Jersey, and learn how real people live."

"Next time…hmmmm, I like the sound of that." She perched up on his chest to study his face. The light was almost non-existent, but she didn't need it. Her fantasy man wasn't a hazy figment in her head anymore. The details were being filled in, her own Sam-portrait in progress.

There was the slightly crooked left eyebrow that most of his viewing audience assumed was his intelligent, quizzical look, but seeing him relaxed, even sleeping, she now realized it just grew that way. His lashes were golden-tipped, although she didn't dare tell him that, because he would think it was girly. Then there was the way he brushed his hand through his hair when he was thinking, and didn't know anyone was watching.

Mercedes was always watching. She ran her hands

up over his torso, twirling a finger in the chest hair. The golden-tipped lashes opened, and sated green (not hazel) eyes gleamed.

"Let's not rush past 'this time,'" he said. "The night isn't over."

"I could stay like this forever."

He sighed, and she could feel the slow rise and fall of his chest beneath her. "See, this is how I know that what you write is fiction. I have no warm spot on this couch. Don't you have a bed?"

"It's a Murphy bed, and I don't usually fold it out, and you were in a hurry."

He started to laugh. "I should've guessed. This place suits you."

"I'm a wreck?"

"No, your priorities aren't the same as normal people," he said, softening the words with a kiss to her hair.

They stayed there quietly, and she wondered why she'd never appreciated the steely security of a man's arms before, the curve of his bicep, the hard lines of his chest. Lying here with Sam, the view out the window looked like paradise dusted in stars, rather than a rusted fire escape. Tonight her old couch was the most perfect place in the world. Sam stirred, their legs tangled together in a knot she was in no hurry to untie.

"Are you hungry?"

"Food?" he asked, his hand sweeping over the curve of her back, up and over, long, languid strokes.

"Ziti, in particular," she answered. If she moved just an inch to the left…

"Maybe in a minute. I'm treasuring my warm spot here."

"You're making fun again."

"Only because you make me smile."

"How was the interview with the law professor?"

"Pretty sharp. He had some good case points on capital punishment. The Supreme Court has got a case in a few months, we'll see what happens."

"We could turn the television on to watch the show."

"Bite your tongue. I'm quite happy here."

"Short sofa and all."

"It's the 'all' part that I'm happy about."

"What kept you tonight?"

"A meeting with Charlie."

"What was that?"

"What?"

"It was not an enthusiastic answer. Like it was a really bad meeting and you just don't want to whine."

"I don't mind whining, but it was actually a good meeting."

"So why the lack of enthusiasm?"

"I'm enthusiastic."

"That's not enthusiasm. That's brooding."

"I don't brood."

"Morose. Melancholy. Down in the dumps. Life in the crapper. Pick a word, any word."

"I didn't want to say anything yet—"

"Aha! It was a bad meeting."

"No, it was good. But things are going to change."

"Good change or bad change?"

"It depends on your point of view."

"Just tell me."

"I'm running for Congress. One of the candidates has dropped out at the last minute. They want me in," he said.

"Oh! Oh." Congress. Just the word gave her hives.

Sam studied her face. "What do you think?"

"Are you serious?" she asked, but she knew he was. It was wonderful, it was daunting, it scared her senseless.

"Yeah. I met with the party chairman and a campaign manager yesterday. What do you think?"

"Wait a minute."

Mercedes reluctantly disengaged from his arms and fumbled through her purse. Then she came back, and handed him a twenty-dollar bill.

"If you're running for Congress, I want a lifetime tax exemption for Mercedes Brooks. No, that's too selfish. I want one for the entire Brooks family—except for Andrew. With his money, the pork police would be all over you."

He looked down at the twenty. "I can't do that."

She folded up the bill and smiled. "Okay, you passed. You're not for sale. I like that in my elected representatives."

"That's all you have to say?"

She climbed up on him, and happily engaged herself back in his arms. "You're nervous about this, aren't you?"

"Yeah."

"Why?"

"What if I lose?"

"Sam, that'd be like George Washington losing, or Abraham Lincoln losing, or Thomas Jefferson losing. Of course you're going to win."

"Those are all dead guys. Name a guy who's still alive."

She stayed silent.

"What's wrong?"

"You're the only non-dead guy I know of that's a shoo-in to win. Oh, my God. I'd be sleeping with a member of Congress. Assuming you still want to sleep with me after you win."

"The election's three months away. I've got a lot of campaigning to catch up on."

"Oh, yeah, make me feel better." Then she broached the one issue that was forecasting rain for her parade. "Campaigning?"

"Yeah."

"Oh."

"Don't 'oh,'" he said, and she could hear the worry in his voice.

This was his shining moment, and she was raining on not only her parade, but his as well. Mercedes smiled at him, shoving her own problems to tomorrow when she'd be alone.

"I think you'll make a great Congressman, Sam Porter. The people of New York couldn't ask for anything better."

"New Jersey."

"What do you mean, New Jersey?"

"I live in Jersey. That's my home state."

"But what about the people of New York? Don't we deserve honest representatives, too?" It was one thing when he was going to be her Congressman, but he was going to be someone else's Congressman, not hers?

"New York has good representatives."

"But not as good as you, Sam. We deserve the best."

"Move to Jersey."

She snuggled closer, because New York's loss was New Jersey's gain, but right at the moment, she was the one laying naked with him. "No way."

"Yeah, I can see how all your creature comforts

would be so appealing," he said, his hand moving lower with nefarious intentions.

"You're mocking me," she said, but the words had no sting because his nefarious intentions were no longer just intentions. One finger teased between her thighs, circling and stroking, feather-light touches that slipped higher and higher.

Sam switched their positions, so she was flat on her back. He straddled over her, diamond-sharp eyes watching as he teased with his hand. The noise of the city faded to nothing, her senses focused on the sound of his breathing, the touch of his hand, the musky smell of arousal in the air.

The steadfast touch continued, sliding in between her wet crease, circling, then sliding further, her hips rolling upwards to meet him. He would touch her just so, not enough, never enough.

Then he waited, and a moan broke free from her lips at the loss. His lips curved up in a smile, all male, all knowing, as if she were his puppet on a string, but oh, he knew exactly which strings to pull.

The ache inside her was growing, and she moaned restlessly, wanting to come, but every time she was close, he would pull back, and the torment would start all over again.

Back and forth, back and forth. Her head moved from side to side, words coming from her mouth, cursing him because she needed to come so badly, and all he would do was laugh. A soft, whisper of a laugh that skimmed over her body, over her breasts, settling in her mind, thudding in her clit.

His lips came down over hers, his tongue thrusting

inside her, and as her hips ground against his finger, his
tongue made love in her mouth. The thrill of him, his
mouth, his hand, his touch, took her up and up, so close
to falling, so close….

This time, he knew, and was merciful. The lovely,
lovely finger moved faster and faster against her, and she
was so ready to come. There. There.

But then it wasn't his finger any more. He thrust his
cock inside her, his mouth still covering hers, and the
pure relief was instant. Her thighs clamped against him
while he moved deep and strong, and the first flush of
the orgasm rolled through her. Tension radiated from
him, muscles corded, and slick with sweat. He raised his
head, stared, and she fell deeply into his eyes at the same
time the climax took over. So much there, so strong, so
gentle, so perfect.

When she moaned, it didn't come from her body,
but her heart.

The flame from the candle blurred in front of her
eyes, a prism of colors emerging from the fire. He rode
her to his own completion, and then fell still.

She wanted to believe it was only sex between them,
it would be easier for him, for her. But "only sex" didn't
explain the tenderness in his face, "only sex" didn't
explain the hopes in her mind, "only sex" didn't explain
why even the afterwards with Sam was better than the
during of her other encounters.

Long moments passed, the sound of breathing, the
city noises taking hold, cars honking, the quiet hiss of
the candle flames. Yet all Mercedes could hear was the
steady bump of his heart.

Sam was everything a man should be. Honest, caring,

reliable, give or take an hour, and most of all, he was the most honorable man she'd ever known. Every night he told the entire country what he believed in, taking the hits in stride, but never letting it stop him from what he thought was right. People didn't do that anymore, they were too afraid.

Mercedes let out a sigh, because honest, caring and reliable men didn't belong with her. He heard her sigh, misread the reason, and rolled her back on top of him.

"Sam, this campaigning business, will I still be able to see you? It's going to be worse, isn't it?"

"I'm not going anywhere. I found my warm spot, all three-quarters of an inch of it, and I'm not giving it up. It'll be worse for a while. But then it's over. We'll work it out. Promise."

"Okay."

"No brooding."

"I'm not brooding."

"Don't make problems, Mercedes. I don't have to run."

At that, she raised her head, jamming a hard fist into his chest. "Don't you dare not do this, Sam Porter. America needs you." I need you, too, she thought, keeping the words quiet in her heart. "What would you do?"

"If I won?"

"Not if, but when. Let's be realistic."

"You're good for my ego, Mercedes."

"This isn't about ego, this is about doing your patriotic duty for your country. What would you do?"

His chest rumbled with laughter. "There're a few heads in the House that have some common sense. I'd work with them. Budget needs help, foreign diplomacy needs help. That's where I'd start."

"You could do a lot."

"Washington is a lot like Wonderland. You've got to be careful not to drink the water, or who knows how you end up."

"Hmmm."

"What are you thinking?"

"Just thinking," she answered. She didn't know much about the political process, but like it or not, she was about to get a baptism by fire. It would have been nice if they'd been together a little longer first. Like maybe a month.

"No brooding."

"I'm not brooding."

"So I have a question for you."

"What?"

"Do you really keep chocolate sauce in your refrigerator?"

"No. That's just fiction."

"Ah. It's a good thing I brought some, then."

BY THE NEXT AFTERNOON, Mercedes had written an online profile for Tony and e-mailed it to Sam, posted two mediocre stories for her Web site, written three yuck pages on her next manuscript, played seven games of Solitaire, and had viewed an anonymous sex video that some Wall Street trader had sent her in hopes of getting it posted on her blog. In response, Mercedes sent him her standard form rejection letter:

I'm sorry, but although your efforts showed promise, we find your submission not quite what we're looking for. I didn't feel the enthusiasm for the project that I should have. Thank you for your interest, and best of luck in your sex video career.

Mercedes Brooks
Coming in 2008, *The Return of the Red Choo Diaries*

This time, when she hit the send button, she didn't get her usual charge of satisfaction. In fact, she didn't get a charge at all. Sadly, her attention was fixated on the pillow in her lap. She picked it up, inhaling deeply. Sam's cologne. She'd walked to the Starbucks that morning, and right after she crossed 14th street, the scent had hit her nose. She turned, ready to see him, but it was just some doofus who had the nerve to wear Sam Porter's cologne. Ruined her whole morning.

Maybe if she did a story about a man's cologne, and the woman who dabs it on herself in order to be able to smell her lover on her when he wasn't there? She was struck by inspiration, felt the need to run to Sak's and buy a bottle of his cologne, when cooler heads (and lack of funds) prevailed and she sat down to write.

When the phone rang, a few minutes later, her first thought was Sam. Her second thought, as she glanced at CallerID was Portia. Her excitement dimmed.

"Doll, great news!"

Okay, it was a nice way to start. "Portia, tell me more."

"What do the words 'second printing' say to you?"

"I can pay next month's rent."

Portia laughed. "You're such a card."

"Forget compliments, tell me about the printing."

"The warehouse is out of stock. Apparently your book has started to fly off the shelves, apparently with the

Victoria's Secret slash book club crowd. Who knew? Anyway, just wanted to share the love. The head of PR is trying to line up an interview with you on one of the talk shows. Just think. All that exposure. Your face would be plastered everywhere. Instant recognition, doll."

Instant recognition? But she liked her anonymity. For instance, she could go out with whomever she chose to (Sam) and not worry about him being linked with a well-known writer of erotica. "Maybe I should play it low-key. Right now, I'm pretty faceless, which can be a good thing when you write erotica." Or date a Congressional candidate. Or both.

"Well, yeah, but that's your big hook. You're gorgeous, and you're willing to go out there, and stand up for what you're writing. Not trying to hide behind some fake pen name. People like that. It makes you seem real, earthy, yet sexually charged, too."

"Sexually charged is good."

"How's the next book coming?"

"Slow."

"Doll, when you're writing sex, slow is a definite plus."

"Thanks, Portia."

"Loved you on the Sam Porter show, by the way. He's such a hottie."

"Thank you for watching."

"I've heard he's a hard-ass in person, is that true?"

Yes, he does have a hard ass. "I thought he was very personable, but what do I know?"

"Oh, yeah, those talking-head types. I'll be in touch. Kisses."

Mercedes hung up and returned to her writing.

For a maintenance man, he had the nicest smell, a combination of cologne, soap and some other elusive something that made her want to lean in and inhale. She pretended an interest in the work he was doing under the sink, and her breasts rubbed against his back. He turned, looked at her, his eyes darkening. She rose quickly, embarrassed by what she'd done, and he went back to his work, leaving her to study his ass. And a nice ass it was. Hard, firm, just made for a woman's hands as he penetrated deep inside her....

_11_

SAM DIDN'T BOTHER driving to Jersey the next morning. He snuck into the studio, showered, changed, and was working at his desk before anyone noticed. He looked over the dating profile that Mercedes had written for Tony, and was really impressed.

"Tony, it's Sam."

"Yeah."

"Listen, got a profile done for you."

"A profile for what?"

"Internet dating."

"I don't need a dating profile, Sam."

"No, no, this could work. You should use it. Or at least read it. I think it'd be good for you."

"What if no one wants to meet me?"

"Ah, Tony. Don't do this to yourself. Read it."

"You wrote this for me?"

"Nah. A friend did it."

"You told a stranger about my situation?"

"Don't get upset. She's nice."

"She?"

"Yeah. She."

"She thinks I should, huh?"

"Definitely."

"Does this she have a name, Sam?"

"You'll meet her on Saturday."

"Uh-huh. You have a girlfriend, don't you, Sam? I'm going out with you two and I'll be stuck as the third wheel, won't I?"

"It's not that way, Tony."

"What? No girlfriend, or no third wheel."

"She's not exactly my girlfriend."

"Jeez, Sam."

"Will you trust me?"

"Only because it's you."

"Everything's going to be fine. Really."

After he hung up, Kristin came in, bearing a box.

"Delivery. This is like the sixth box you've had sent here these past few days. What are you doing? Moving your stuff in one package at a time?"

"It's research for a project I'm working on." He stood up. "Need help with that?"

"Uh, yeah, about five minutes ago."

Sam took the box from her and moved it to the pile behind his desk. Kristin eyed the boxes. "I'm hoping those are the crew's Christmas presents."

Sam chose not to burst her bubble. "You could think that. What's the latest on Friedman? Did we get him for Friday?"

Kristin nodded. "He's a go."

"Good."

She stared at him curiously. "You okay?"

"Never better. What's wrong?"

"You forgot to shave, Sam. You never forget to shave."

Sam rubbed his jaw, felt the stubble there. *Damn* "Whoops. Middle age, huh?"

Kristin wasn't buying it. "Right."

After she left, Sam went back and shaved, and this time checked in the mirror. Better. He was listening to the White House press briefing when Franco stopped by, settling into the chair across from Sam's desk.

Sam turned the tape off. "What?"

"We don't talk anymore."

Sam stared in confusion. "What the heck? I called you four days ago."

"And you didn't think ignoring my advice was worth a mention? I tell you, Sam, I don't know what's going on with you. Ignoring your friends, politics. What's next? Cosmetic surgery? You're running for Congress?"

"Yes. Yes, I am," he stated. Definitely. For the record. Two words that would change the direction of his life. Forever.

Franco pondered that. "Okay."

"That's all you have to say?"

"It'd be okay."

"You said it'd be a big mistake when I asked you about it earlier."

"True. But that's the best way to deal with you."

"Then why the drama, if this isn't that big of a deal?"

Franco waved a hand. "I just like to see you squirm. That's all. So what else is happening in your life that I should know about?"

"You're just coming in, making me squirm, and then say 'hey, how's life?'"

"Yeah, that pretty much sums it up."

Sam blew out a breath. "Franco, you've changed. You're more useless than you used to be."

"I have only one word. Mandy."

"How long have you known her?"

"Almost six weeks."

"Six weeks? Is that all?"

"Yes. What's the problem?"

"I think that as mature men we should consider things rationally, weigh all sides, and come to a reasonable conclusion. We should not jump into bed with somebody because she's hot and our dick is aching. Understand what I'm saying?"

"No."

"How old are you, Franco? Forty-two, forty-three?"

"Thirty-nine."

"And how old is this Mandy-person?"

"Twenty-eight."

"Thirteen years, my friend. Thirteen years. When she was eleven, you were twenty-four. When she was listening to N-Sync, you were listening to Pink Floyd. She probably doesn't even have a defined career yet. She's thinking about making a name for herself, and you're past that. Can she even pick out China on a map, Franco? Answer me that."

"Of course she knows where China is, she works in a newsroom. And there's only eleven years between us, not thirteen."

"But it could be thirteen, and that's even worse. And think about this. What do you know about her belief system, what if she cheats on her income tax, and you get married, and then two years down the road you're both in jail, because you jumped into a relationship too fast. Oh, sure, she makes you happy, makes you laugh and all, and pulls you out of the funk you've been in, but is that enough?"

"Sam, have you been to a therapist about this? I think you're working too hard. Slow down, get some rest. The stress is starting to affect you."

"We're in this together, Franco. The whole male sex is in a downward slide into a dark pit of mud where *Girls Gone Wild* tapes loop endlessly in our heads. It's Darwin in reverse."

"Sam, do me a favor. Go out, do what every other man does when he starts talking weird. Buy a new car. Something red, flashy, like what Letterman drives."

"I don't need a new car, Franco."

"You need a lobotomy, is what you need."

A lobotomy wouldn't fix it. Mercedes was stuck in his head, stuck in a place where even medical science couldn't take her away. He knew it. Just like he knew the grass was green, the sky was blue, and if the liberals had their way, they would raise the capital gains tax again. "You think two people can just meet and boom— it's there?"

"It depends on your definition of the word 'it.'"

"A relationship. A stable, long-lasting relationship built on mutual respect of another human being, not just endless hours in bed."

"I don't know. That's a tough one. If you're spending endless hours in bed, who needs talk?"

Sam tapped his finger on the desk. "This is exactly my point, Franco. We should demand talk time. That's what separates us from the animals."

"No one has ever ascertained what separates us from animals. People say thought, people say language, people say religion, and people say arrogance. You know why there's no consensus, Sam? Because there is no difference. We are animals. We should accept it and move on, and if that means dating a hot twenty-eight-year-old and spending hours in bed, rather than quality talk time, I'm all for it."

"You are an animal, Franco," said Sam.

"Thank you."

After Franco left, Sam decided that he had to accept some facts. He wasn't going through a midlife crisis at thirty-nine. That'd been a knee-jerk reaction to the mind-blogging, fact-defying, age-defying intensity of his feelings for Mercedes. Lust was there, yes, but other things, too. Respect, admiration, and companionship. The way he wanted her with him every day. The way he wanted to talk to her about things. The way he wanted to make her smile.

Time to accept the change of course, and move on.

He wanted Mercedes. He wanted her for keeps.

SAM PICKED HER UP AFTER the show on Tuesday and drove her into Jersey. Along the drive on the Palisades, he gave her a guided tour, which helped to calm Mercedes's nerves. It wasn't that Sam was a scary driver, it was the idea of being in a car, going to his house. He had a house. It smacked of permanency, and permanency made her nervous, because permanency didn't last.

"Now, I know it's dark and you can't see, so you'll have to trust me on the scenery that is passing by. New Yorkers like to make fun, but in New Jersey, this is what we call trees. Grass. Foliage."

"I've seen trees before," said Mercedes snarkily, but it was a nice snark.

"And if you'll listen carefully, you'll hear a new sound. Silence."

"I can't hear silence when you're talking, Sam."

"Well, if I wasn't talking, you would hear it, and possibly enjoy it."

"That's why you're a talk show host, isn't it? You live alone, and you like to talk, and there's nobody out in Jersey that will listen, ergo—The Sam Porter show."

"Are you insulting me?"

"No." Mercedes sighed. "I'm just all tied up in knots about this thing."

"It's not a 'thing.' It's a relationship."

"It's an affair," she stated.

Sam gave her a hard look. "I like 'thing' better. On your left, you will notice a gas station, which is used to provide cars with fuel at a significantly cheaper price than some other states—not to be specific, New York—which use taxes as a club to regulate behaviors."

"I don't know."

"I'm very stubborn, Mercedes. 'Bull-dogged temperament' is what the *Washington Post* said. You can't argue with the *Post*."

She leaned her head back against the leather interior, and listened for the silence. He reached out and touched her cheek. For tonight, just for one night, she was going to believe.

SHE HADN'T KNOWN WHAT TO expect from Sam's house. Her imagination had fluctuated between a log cabin in the woods, to a McMansion complete with gold fountain in the front. The actual habitat surprised her. Pleasantly. The driveway curved into a forest of fir trees, fenced off from the rest of the world. The house was a cute Colonial, almost hidden from the trees, two gables perched at the top, and a cobblestone walk leading to the front entrance.

Sam parked in the garage and took her hand.

"Ready?" he asked.

Oh, God. He had a garage. Mercedes gathered every bit of her courage and nodded.

He opened the door, and immediately there was barking.

"Down, Max. You're not allergic to dogs, are you?"

Mercedes took in the medium-sized Lab, the earnest dark eyes, the floppy ears, the bobbing tail, and sighed. Oh, God, he had a dog.

She reached out a hand, patted the black furry head, and his pink tongue reached out and licked her hand.

Sam smiled. "Dog's not stupid. I'll give you the tour," he said, and he did. There was a living room, a dining room (he said it was mainly unused), and a kitchen that was bigger than her apartment. He had a laundry room that actually dented through her fear. The idea of no longer having to cart her laundry out. Okay, that was cool.

Then there was the office. And at least four bathrooms. They went down into the basement, where he showed her the game room.

"I can't believe you have a game room," she said, staring at the billiard table, pinball machine, huge couch and flat-panel TV.

Sam shrugged his shoulders, looking almost embarrassed. "When I was a kid, everybody else had a basement that was the rec room. I always wanted a rec room. Now I have one."

"You are one big kid, aren't you?"

"I'm an adult."

She laid her hand on the glass of the Black Knight game. "This is a pinball machine. Do you have any nieces or nephews? Cousins?"

"I have two nieces that go to school in California."

"This is all for you?"

"Maybe." She shook her head.

"Oh, Sam." She walked over the pool table in the corner, the Tiffany light hanging overhead. "You good at pool?"

"Yeah. You?"

"No."

"Great, we'll play for stakes of clothing later. Want to see the pool?"

"You have a pool?"

He nodded, and led her upstairs. On the back of the house, facing to the backyard was a windowed room, covered in green plants, and exotic flowers. In the center was the pool, the water not blue, but the green of a natural lagoon. It was rounded, but long enough for laps. It was gorgeous, and enough to turn a die-hard New Yorker into a New Jersey fan for life.

"Is it heated?"

"Yeah."

"You swim?"

"At night. Good exercise, nice way to relax. With the hours at work, I come home stressed out. You like it?"

"Yeah. I like," she answered, feeling her nerves begin to unwind. Just one night, she kept repeating to herself, her eyes watching the hypnotic flow of the lights underneath the water. Just for tonight, she'd believe.

"Do you swim?"

"Not very well."

"That's okay. I won't let you drown. Promise."

"I didn't bring a suit."

"Why would you need one?'

AFTER DINNER, SHE SETTLED next to him on the couch, and this was no ordinary couch. It was puffy and fluffy and seated forty, as compared to her small Murphy bed, which only seated one on a good day.

He was just promising to show her his etchings when the phone rang.

"Hey, Martin. Yeah, this is a bad time. What did you need?

"No, can't tonight. What for?

"A campaign speech? Already?

"Well, yes, I know the election's coming up, and I did assume there would be campaigning, only I didn't think about it so soon.

"Where?

"I can be there. You don't mind if I bring a friend?" he said, looking in her direction.

Mercedes scowled. Sam scowled back. "Or two? My business manager and his date.

"Yeah. Sounds great. I'll put you down for breakfast this week.

"Thanks," he said, and hung up. "Sorry about that."

"It's okay. You're a busy guy," she murmured.

He sat down next to her, pulled her close. "This would be much easier if you weren't pasty white with fright. You're lucky that my ego is as big as it is."

"That was your campaign manager?"

"Yeah. Martin. He's everything you think a campaign manager should be. Smooth, well-funded, and always willing to change opinions on a dime."

"When are you going to announce to the world that you're running?"

"Early next week. Monday. Martin's setting up the press conference now."

"He's good?"

"The best," he said sadly.

"You deserve the best."

"I have the best," he told her, his eyes intent before stealing a kiss.

Mercedes let herself go, let herself float away on the pleasure of his mouth. He undressed her, and she thought they would make love on the couch. Easy enough. But Sam had other ideas. He picked her up and carried her to the pool, setting her down in the shallow end. Quickly he shed his clothes, and she watched, because he was such a beautiful man to her. His body was long, with shoulders that were made to pillow her head, a wide chest tapering to narrow hips. Long legs. And then there was his sex…

He came into the water, and guided her in. It was heavenly soft and warm against her skin. So easy to float away.

"Twelve months ago when you were on the show, I wanted to see you like this. All that dark hair floating in the water. Nipples teasing the surface. Your eyes looking, gleaming up at me. I wanted to have you here, Mercedes."

His hands skimmed over her breasts, over her shoulders, drawing her closer. He kissed her in the water, slowly, soothing, and she couldn't resist. She could never resist him. Never resist the things that he promised with his eyes.

He made love to her in the water, everything warm, light, weightless. Here there were no worries. Here, she didn't need to think about the tomorrows. Afterwards, he bundled her in a fluffy towel and led her to bed. She lay down next to him, curled in his arms. She was so tired of fighting her feelings, so tired of pretending she didn't care. She cared.

She loved.

12

THE NEXT MORNING, MERCEDES woke up to nothing but a Sam-sized dent on the pillow next to her. She stretched out on the bed, amazed at how far an arm could actually extend in a king-size bed. She kept scooching and reaching over the side, like Christopher Columbus, just to see how far it was before she found the new world, and her hand eventually dropped off the edge. She wiggled her fingers in the air, and was rewarded with a wet lick of a tongue on her palm. Mercedes lifted her head, opened her eyes, and peeked.

Max wagged his tail at her, hope shining in his dark eyes.

"Good morning, Max. I suppose you're hungry."

His tail wagged even faster.

Next to her pillow was a note from Sam.

Your computer is in the office. Feel free to use whatever you need. The cleaning lady comes around lunch time, but I normally hide in the basement, and she ignores me. You may be braver. I'll be home early. Nobody important on the show tonight, so I'll be there by seven.

Mercedes kept rereading the words over and over. It was no declaration of love, but in many ways, it was scarier. He was establishing her here at his house, as if she belonged. It wouldn't be hard to belong here, she thought to herself, picking up his pillow, holding it close.

Max looked at her, and barked.

"You're laughing at me, aren't you? I know."

She sighed, and started to get out of bed, but she wasn't dressed. She looked at Max and considered. Mercedes was something of a dog novice, and she debated the effect of female nudity on a dog's fragile psyche, but eventually concluded that she was being ridiculous.

She got up, and went to the window, looking outside at the trees. Max followed her, sniffing.

Mercedes stared balefully. "Horny like your owner, aren't you? Can you go away while I get dressed?"

Max barked.

"Yeah, Sam wouldn't have bought that either. Fine, just grow up to be damaged goods, but don't rat me out, huh?"

She threw on some clothes and wandered through the house. It felt strange being in a house, not weird strange, but unfamiliar strange. She'd lived her entire life in an apartment, and never thought twice about it. But this…

He wasn't kidding about the trees and the foliage. The leaves were beginning to turn for fall, green and gold and brown, all mixed together, colors as far as the eye could see.

And the quiet. A writer could get some serious work done out here, with nothing but trees, and one hungry dog.

"Where's your food?" she asked, and he led her out to the door between the kitchen and the garage.

She opened the door, and Max ran out into the

garage. She looked around, and then noticed the rows upon rows of boxes lined up neatly against the wall. There must have been two or three hundred boxes there, all the same. And familiar.

Mercedes went over to one, looked at the label. These were her books. Thousands of copies.

Oh.

Her hand lifted to her chest, because her heart was filling so quickly, and she knew it would burst. Knew that no small organ could contain that much and survive. She stayed there stupidly frozen, one hand to her heart.

He'd done this for her. Mercedes.

Sam Porter, America's conservative talk show host, had bought over ten thousand copies of a book that some people considered pornographic. He hadn't done it for a sexual thrill. He'd done it for her.

THAT NIGHT, SAM CAME HOME to a dark house. His first thought was that Mercedes had left, but then he saw the candles flickering on the table, and he smelled the aroma of something warm and Italian.

"Hello, Sam," she said, and he turned to see her, not nearly prepared for the sight of Mercedes standing in his kitchen, holding a wooden spoon, and wearing—nothing.

"I looked for an apron, but you didn't have any, so I improvised."

He nodded stupidly.

"Why don't you sit down and eat?" she asked in a husky voice that slid down his spine.

Obediently Sam sat.

She put down a plate of food in front of him, and he wasn't sure what it was, because he could feel her nipples burning a hole in his back. She handed him a fork, and then sat in the chair next to him, long dark hair falling over her breasts, her legs slightly parted, exposing a dark, downy triangle, and Sam, finally unable to deny what his cock was crying for, put down his fork with resolute purpose.

He had priorities; food wasn't one of them.

When he stood, she pushed a hand against him in mock protest. "No, not yet."

"You've got to be kidding."

"No," she answered, and turned to walk away. His eyeballs were glued to her bouncy butt hypnotizing him with the sexy pitch and roll.

Having no choice, Sam followed.

She took him over to the couch, and with a one-finger press knocked him down. Then her hands were at his fly, pushing at his jeans. She reached beneath his boxers and freed him, her hands cupping him, stroking, and Sam groaned from the velvet touch. She licked her lips, slowly, deliberately, and leaned over and took him in her mouth. He shuddered in relief at the softness of her lips, the cunning of her tongue. She was thorough, sending him beyond reason. He knew he was close to coming, and he didn't want to, didn't want to. He pulled back, but her hands held him down, her lips moved down further on his cock, and he had no choice. He shuddered from the intensity, and Mercedes took from him, her mouth sucking hard, until he had nothing more to give.

IT TOOK A MOMENT FOR SAM to recover, but when he did, the green eyes (not hazel) were lit with wicked intent. Mercedes arched a brow.

He shook his head slowly.

Mercedes took a step back, preparing to flee.

Sam swept her up in his arms, Rhett Butler to her Scarlett, and took her to the bedroom, where he dumped her on the bed.

"What was that for?"

He put a finger to her lips. "Don't talk."

He was back in a moment, lying down on top of her, pulling her hands over her head. He kissed her then, a fierce, opened-mouth kiss that took her by surprise. He probed her with his tongue, one knee parting her thighs, and she moaned into his mouth. She pulled at her hands, wanting to touch him, hold him, but his hands were tight on her wrist. Her blood pumped like hot oil, pouring fire through her veins.

There was a wildness about him that she'd never known before, and it called to an answering wildness within her. Her body was throbbing with need, and she rubbed against the hard ridge of his flesh, desperate to have him. His mouth clamped down on one nipple, sucking hard, and Mercedes nearly flew off the bed. Oh, it was almost painful, but such a perfectly beautiful pain. All she wanted was to relieve that ache. Relieve that pain. Her back arched, and she stretched, finding….

…her hands were tied to the bed.

Sam smiled. "Payback," he said, in that beautifully modulated voice. A voice that on its own could bring her to orgasm at certain times—like now.

He kissed her again, not quite so fierce, but she still could feel the edge inside him. His lips suckled against her neck, against her ear, whispering words she wanted to hear. Then he moved to her breasts again, pulling, and she felt liquid pools of pleasure, dripping within her. Inside her. Around her. Through her.

She kicked up against him, but found his cock instead, and she nestled against him, wanting to feel him inside her. Around her. Through her.

His lips moved down lower, his tongue trailing over her skin, shooting sensation wherever he stroked. His hand parted her thighs, her folds slick and plump, waiting…. His tongue traced up her thigh, his stubble rasping against her skin, hard against soft. She wanted so much, wanted his mouth, wanted his touch, wanted him. All the want piling inside her, waiting…

Ice. He touched her with his tongue, and she nearly flew out of her skin. His mouth was so cold, so liquid, so painfully beautiful. He had ice. He sucked against her clit, slower now, but the cold was making her shake, making her shudder. She rolled against him, needing this, needing to come, and he stroked again, the water mingling with her own juices, and he held her close, pulling her over, pulling her over, pulling her over the edge.

THAT WEEKEND, HE TOOK HER up to his cabin on Lake George, their last time alone before the press conference on Monday. Mercedes didn't want to think about the looming complications, and actually not thinking about it fit well into her current emotional platform: One day at a time. Not in a relationship. Someday he'll be gone, but this isn't it.

The cabin sat on the east side of the lake, reclusive, and set far from the main road, with several miles of woods in all directions. No doubt about it, Sam liked his privacy. When they pulled up the long, gravel drive,

Mercedes eyed the rustic structure nervously, but after they went inside, she was pleasantly surprised.

"What? You expected post-1970s *Deliverance?*"

Mercedes blushed. "I expected something less comfortable."

And it was comfortable. There was a huge cedar and stone fireplace that ran to the ceiling. Great beams spanned the top of the room. The floor was wooden, covered in a woolen Indian rug, and the walls were sparsely covered in old landscape photos. "No hunting trophies? Deer heads, stuffed bears?"

"They don't impress the ladies."

It should have been a joke, should have made her laugh. Instead it ticked her off, pricked at her insides like ten thousand tiny needles. "So you take all the ladies up here?"

"You're the first," he said, the words thrilling her and scaring her all at the same time.

"The first ever ever?"

"My mom came here when she was alive. So, if you want to be precise, you're the second female."

"Precise is important," answered Mercedes, trying to ignore the supremely satisfied look on his face, and she wondered if she'd fallen into a skillfully executed mind-trap. They had tea on the couch, made love in front of the fireplace, and Mercedes fell asleep wrapped up in his arms.

The next morning, he woke her up at five. In the morning, not the evening. Mercedes whapped him in the chest. "It's too early."

"Not for the fish. Come on. You're the second female to be up here with me, don't make me second-guess my decision."

"Blackmail is a very low tactic, Sam."

"But effective?"

She glared. "But effective."

"Dress in warm stuff. It gets cold out there."

A small boat was docked a good walk from the house, and he explained the basics of the sport, although she drew the line at baiting her own hook.

Once on the lake, everything was quiet, the wind blowing through the trees. He didn't take them very far out, the cove was fairly small, and although she could hear some boat motors in the distance, nothing came close. Just the two of them on the water, the boat rocking gently.

"How long does it take to catch a fish?" she asked, getting used to the feel of the rod and reel in her hands.

"However long it takes. But the point of fishing is not to catch fish.

"Ah. Silly me. All those poor, misguided fishermen."

"You know what the point is?"

"You're going to tell me?"

"It's hearing the quiet lapping of the water, seeing the blue of the sky, listening to the wind rustle through the leaves. It gives you time to think. People don't think enough."

"There's no blue in that sky. Just fast-moving clouds."

"We'll have rain soon. But for now we fish."

"And think," she reminded him. "What do you think about?"

"Whatever I want. Peace in the Middle East or what I want for dinner."

"Deep stuff."

"Not always."

"Does it bother you if I talk to you while you fish?" she asked, watching the dark clouds bearing lower in the sky.

"Nah."

"But I don't have to."

"Mercedes, you can say what you want."

"Right now, you have your show, and tens of millions of people listen to you every day, and they listen to what you say, and you know how much influence that is? And when you get to Washington, because I know you'll get to Washington, then suddenly your influence dives down to 435 WASP-y men, of which only fifty percent would give you the time of day, so now we're down to 217, give or take a few seats, and they all have their own agendas to push, so you're really only one voice in 435, versus one voice that's influencing tens of millions. Isn't that a step down for you?"

"Very deep question for five-thirty in the morning."

"Thank you, I do my best thinking in the morning."

"I'll remember that, but to start with, my viewing audience isn't close to tens of millions, we're still in the single digit million numbers—"

"But still sizeable."

He nodded. "Still sizeable. But in my seat in the studio, I can talk, I can whine, I can argue, I can debate, I can opine, but at the end of the day, it's just talk. A man shouldn't be judged only by his words."

"But I get judged only by my words?"

"That's different," he said, as the boat rocked harder, the waves lapping higher against the sides.

"No, it's not. At the end of the day, I don't do anything. I talk on paper. You talk on television. Apples to apples."

He frowned. "Okay, maybe. But it doesn't bother you, does it?"

"Sometimes," she answered, "but I've got lots of time left."

"I don't know, Mercedes. I just get mad, and I want to fix things, and my father taught me that a leaking pipe never got fixed by standing around and talking about it."

"Sheldon's doing something now."

"Summerville?"

"Brooks, thank you very much."

"Sorry."

"S'all right. She's funding music education for kids. What's your stance on public funding for the arts, Sam?"

"To be honest, I haven't thought much about it. Math and science is where most of the emphasis should go."

"But to cut it off completely?"

"You want to have this debate at five-thirty in the morning?"

Mercedes sat up as straight as possible when rocking on water. "Yes, yes, I do."

"You're with Sheldon, I take it."

"I think I am."

"First thing, you have to make a definitive opinion. Not wishy-washy, no fence-straddling. You state your case, your arguments for the cause, and then you stick to it."

"Kids need music. There's causal connections between math and music, and where would the United States be without music? There'd be no "Star-Spangled Banner," no "America the Beautiful," and no Elvis. If you don't stop the cuts in funding for music, that—that'd be esquivalience on your part."

"Esquivalience?"

"I know big words, too. I'm a writer."

"I think you made it up."

"It means the willful avoidance of one's official responsibilities."

"I still think you made it up."

"Look in the dictionary, Sam. I'm highly educated, you know." She smiled, pleased with herself. "So what did you think?"

He nodded with approval. "You did that well."

"Do you find yourself swayed at all?"

"For you, I could be swayed."

"Maybe I should find a cause, too."

Sam made a face. "Here's the thing, Mercedes. If you don't believe in it, really, honestly believe in it, it'll never work. Wait until something finds you, hits you over the head. You're right. You are young."

"But not too young," she reminded him, feeling a fat raindrop on her face.

"Not that young."

"Are you one of those hard-core he-man types who fishes in the rain?"

"Not on your life," he said, and cranked up the motor.

They made it back to the dock as the rain started to fall.

She raced up the path, Sam not far behind, but by the time they were inside, both of them were soaked.

"How fast can you get a fire in that thing?" she asked, pulling off her jacket, shivering from the cold chill of the rain.

"Four minutes, and the clock starts now," he replied, and in short order the flames was blasting heat into the small room.

Mercedes sat closer, hands outstretched. "Much better, and a minute left on the clock."

She watched him then, the heat of the fire lighting his face with a ruddy glow. His hair dripped with moisture, his eyes narrowed, and the air in the room got very still. The rain pounding on the roof, the crackle of the fire, the insanely loud beating of her heart.

"You look like a mermaid, your hair wet like that." He reached out and caught a stand between his fingers.

Her eyes locked on his, and she began to unbutton her shirt. "Clothes are wet," she whispered softly.

"I could help," he offered.

"Let me," she said, sliding the shirt off her shoulders. Underneath her shirt was a plain white T-shirt. His hand reached out, and touched her through the shirt. Then he lowered his head, using his mouth to wet the fabric even more, pulling one tightly beaded nipple into his mouth.

Mercedes bit back a moan, and he hauled her close. It was supposed to have been a slow seduction, but when she was with Sam, slow had left the building. She wanted him with an urgency that never seemed to stop. His hands pulled at her jeans, and she lifted her hips, as he jerked them off her. His hand parted her thighs, pushed inside her like a spear.

She gasped, not with pain. Not nearly from pain.

"You," she managed, her mouth tightly clenched, because she wanted more than this, her body poised on the edge, needing something more. Needing him.

He lowered his jeans, sheathed himself, and then he entered her. Her senses went on alert, the smell of wet wool, the sound of his words whispering against her neck. Her hands pulled at him, needing to touch him, and not buffered through layers of clothes.

There was something raw and primitive about the feel of wood at her back, the hardness of Sam over her, inside her. The rain beat even louder, and she knew that she could scream here, and there were no other tenants, no other neighbors, no one else but Sam. There was no one else in the world but Sam.

Her hands clawed at the buttons on his shirt, needing to feel his flesh against her. Finally, she found the heated skin, and sighed as he pressed against her, flattening her breasts. It was sex as she'd never known before. Ancient and exposed. No cars, no skyscrapers, no lights. Just a man's carnal possession of a woman.

Her hips lifted, and he took her legs, balancing them on his shoulders, thrusting deeper inside her. Mercedes couldn't think, couldn't feel, she only knew him. This breaching of her carefully built defenses. He kept pounding, turning her inside out, and she could no longer deny him.

Mercedes opened her mouth, and screamed.

SAM NOTICED THAT SHE WAS quiet for the rest of the weekend, and he didn't ask her to explain. She would watch him when she thought he wasn't looking, her eyes soft and curious. If he caught her gaze, the look would change to something more womanly, more wicked…more calculated. On Sunday night, he drove her back to her apartment, and kissed her on the forehead. "I'll pick you up tonight after taping is done."

"You have the press conference tomorrow. I don't think that's very smart, Sam. What if reporters are there?"

"I'm running for the House, not the Presidency. And besides, the day I give up my privacy, is the day I'm dead."

"You're being naive."

"Optimistic."

"Naive."

"When a reporter shows up, just let me know. I'll deal with it."

She stopped arguing with him, but he could read the disagreement in her eyes. "There won't be any problems," he said, needing to convince her, only hoping he was right.

MERCEDES watched the press conference from the cold comfort of her own apartment. It wasn't long, a few questions, a few pithy remarks from Sam, and then boom—he'd moved from Sam Porter, ordinary television talk show host, to Sam Porter, the Candidate.

Her stomach clenched up like a fist, and she sat on her couch, and pretended like it wouldn't matter. In the long run, it wouldn't, because there would be no long run. Only a short run. A fire that would eventually burn itself out. Sam would work in Washington, and Mercedes would spend her days writing erotic blog entries about a tawny-haired man with green eyes she wanted to wake with forever.

Oh, God. The f-word.

For the rest of the afternoon, she wrote crappy sexual fantasies that involved no heart. After all, that was her specialty.

He picked her up that night, exactly as he'd promised.

"I saw the press conference. You need a better tie," she said.

"You're going to take me shopping for a new tie?"

"We can't go shopping anymore," she reminded him.

"We can shop again, not that I will, but we could if we wanted, which I don't. What did you think?"

"You're going to win," she answered, looking out the window, watching the trees of New Jersey pass by. He was going to win unless something got in the way. Her.

They didn't talk about it anymore.

She stayed the next few days at his house. She didn't spot any reporters, which made it easier to pretend that there was no campaign. Sam would be gone during the day. Lunches with rotary clubs, teas with the local library. She wanted to see that one, just to watch Sam handle a china teacup, but wisely she stayed away, and every day, when the sun rose up over the small corner of Bergen County where Sam resided, she would find herself a little more entrenched into this world.

She and Max bonded, although she was careful to keep the bathroom door closed when she dressed. She was brewing some tea when she heard her cell ringing.

"Why aren't you home?"

"Hello?"

"This is Sheldon. Where are you?"

"You don't want to know."

Max barked.

"Is that a dog? For seven days people have been looking for you, and you're spending your nights at a place with a dog?"

"There's nothing wrong with dogs."

"I know, but a person with a pet, well, that implies a heart. You don't spend the night with people with hearts."

"I want you to know that you're not a blood relative. Only my brothers can insult me like that."

"I'm sorry."

"Ha. Got you. It's okay. You're learning the ways of the brood."

"Where are you?"

"You were supposed to forget that question."

"Nope, sorry. No forgetting here. I'm dying to know. I've got suspicions."

"I don't want to know about your suspicions."

"You're confirming my suspicions."

"Don't tell Jeff."

"I'll try to resist, but he has ways of making me talk."

"I don't want to hear this, Sheldon."

"Sorry."

"What's the latest on the wedding?"

"Dresses are done."

"Yay!"

"Flowers are not done. Andrew wants to fly in some Hawaiian flower, which Jamie said is ridiculous, that roses and daisies will be beautiful. Jeff and I started a pool on which flowers will be at the altar. Want in?"

"No."

"You don't sound good."

"I'm fine."

"Not being kidnapped, or taken over by pod people?"

"Nope."

"I was watching the news yesterday and saw the new candidate for the House."

"Oh, who's that?"

"We don't have to talk about this, but I thought you'd want to talk about this."

"Was there a purpose to this call?"

"Yes."

"And it is?"

"You promised to do work for me. I expect you at my apartment on Sunday, eleven o'clock."

"'Kay."

"I can't believe you're there."

"We covered that territory already. Anything else?"

"Sordid details?"

"None to share."

"You could write about it in your blog, you know."

"No."

"Damn, Mercedes."

"I'll see you on Sunday.'

"But—"

"Hanging up now."

Mercedes put away her cell and looked into Max's ever-hopeful eyes. "What are we supposed to do?"

And just like she did every morning, she went back into the bedroom, picked up Sam's pillow, held it close, and smiled.

THAT AFTERNOON, THE doorbell rang. Mercedes wanted to answer it, wanted to tell the stupid reporter to get out of Sam's private life, but she didn't. That wouldn't be smart, so she opted not to answer, and hope the unknown door-knocker would go away. Those hopes were dashed when she heard the key in the lock.

"Damn boy doesn't even bother to set the alarm. Somebody's going to rob him blind…"

Mercedes realized that this must be a repairman; he looked like a repairman in his faded work shirt, his greased denims, and the shock of gray hair. She smiled politely. "Hello."

"I'm here about the leak in the shower."

"Yes," said Mercedes, not realizing that Sam had called someone about the leak in the shower.

"Sam's not here?" asked the man.

"No. He's at work."

"When he gets home, you ask him why the hell he called Pete Connelly to fix his shower. I told him he needs to replace that thing. Doesn't have the decency to call his own father for help? What sort of son does that?"

"His father," repeated Mercedes, as the green (not hazel) eyes cut in her direction.

"Yeah. Who're you?"

"I'm the interior decorator."

Sam's father snorted, and Mercedes pretended not to hear.

"You're here to fix the shower?" she repeated, for lack of something more intelligent to say.

"Well, yeah, don't have enough time to stand around chatting."

"I'll get out of your way," she said and rushed to the back of the house.

Immediately she called Sam on her cell. "Your father is here," she whispered into the phone.

"My dad?"

"Your dad."

"Wow."

"Sam, he looks like he knows."

"Knows what?"

"Knows that we've had sex."

"I guess I'll have to make an honest woman out of you then."

"Sam!"

"You can go and hide in the basement. That's what I do when Olga comes to clean."

"It's your father."

"Do you want me to tell him to leave?"

"God, no. He'll think I'm rude."

"I'm sure he'll really like you, Mercedes. Why don't you talk to him?"

"He's a little gruff."

"Yeah, that's my old man. Listen, we're going to meet Tony tonight. Is that okay?"

"We? Me. You. Us?"

"That's an affirmative."

"I don't think this is a good idea, Sam."

"As much as the idea is tempting to me, I can't just keep you tied up in my bedroom forever."

"Can you not joke about bondage when your father is in the house?"

"I thought you liked it."

"I did, but I don't need to talk about it anymore."

"Mercedes, you write erotica. Why can't you have a sensible discussion about sex?"

"Because it's our sex life, and it's not made up."

"You're a very complicated woman. But I'm okay with it. Tell Dad hello."

And he hung up.

IF MERCEDES WAS A MORE discreet human being, she would have hid in the basement until Sam's father was gone, but curiosity finally took hold, and she ventured into the guest bathroom, where Mr. Porter was removing the showerhead from the wall.

"You're Sam's dad?"

"Yup. Some of us tell the truth about who we are."

"You don't think I'm an interior decorator."

Mr. Porter looked at her and snorted with laughter. "Sam?"

Damn. "I probably should have thought of something better."

"I would have," he answered, peering at the spout.

"You must be very proud of him."

"Proud? I suppose so, but that would mean that I had doubts about him, and I don't. We raised him better than that."

"I'm Mercedes Brooks," she said, holding out a hand.

He looked at it, looked at the grease on his palm and nodded. "Sam Porter."

"Wow. There're two of you in the world."

For some reason, Mr. Porter thought that was funny. "He never did like Junior. Call him that sometime if you want to make him mad."

"I don't think I want to make him mad."

"Too early in the relationship?"

"We don't have a relationship," muttered Mercedes.

"Just decorating, huh?" he answered, going back to work. "Not good for a political candidate to be shacking up with an interior decorator."

"We're not shacking up. I have an apartment in the city."

"He shouldn't be in politics anyway. A bunch of do-nothin', money-grubbin' tax-hikers, that's all the politicians are anyway."

"I guess you've influenced his political outlook."

Sam Sr. nodded. "Guess I have."

Mercedes decided to leave Sam's father to his work.

"I don't think Sam will be needing my services for very long, so I don't think it'll affect the campaign."

His father studied her from beneath gray brows, and for a moment, Mercedes saw exactly what Sam would be like fifty years from now. She could see an older version of herself, standing here, arguing with him. Then in a flash the vision was gone.

Sam Sr., green eyes recognizing much more than Mercedes wanted, answered, "We'll see. We'll see."

13

WHILE SAM WAS SPEAKING at a community center in Toms River, Mercedes spent the afternoon writing a story for her blog about a desperate housewife stuck alone in the house, with no one to turn to but the plumber. It wasn't her best work, but she figured it was good enough. Her mind was occupied with other issues.

That evening, when Sam got home from the show, Mercedes decided it was time for a talk. No longer were they just sharing a bed. She was spending days here, plural. Nights here, plural, and now even his father knew it.

If Sam wasn't careful, soon the world would know it, and Mercedes wasn't ready for the nuclear fallout of that. Right now, the only nuclear fallout she had to deal with was her own, and that was more than enough. They weren't co-habiting, but it was that leaving your toothbrush moment, and Mercedes had never left a toothbrush anywhere but her own bathroom sink. Not even when visiting her mother.

There were certain boundaries that she didn't want to cross, and a toothbrush indicated permanence to the situation. It indicated that tomorrow would come, and they would still be together. Her toothbrush would be where she left it, and Sam would be where she left him as well.

And in the current environment, it would make sense that she went back to her own apartment.

She followed him into the kitchen, and watched as he fed Max.

"How did the speech go this afternoon?"

"Good."

"Good is great," she said, trying her best to be happy and enthusiastic. Sam saw through it.

"What's on your mind?"

"I don't think I should leave my toothbrush."

He looked at her, puzzled. "You don't need to leave your toothbrush. I've already bought you a toothbrush."

"What about my clothes?"

Sam grinned.

"Not funny," she answered.

"Definitely not funny, and I should have known better than to convey levity on such a pressing issue. But actually, your nudity is not an issue, not because it's not a very seductive issue, but because you have clothes here. And while we're on the subject of clothes, I don't know if you realize it or not, but shopping is much cheaper in Jersey. Head out to the mall, the sales tax rate on clothing and shoes sold in New Jersey is zero. Zero. What's it in New York? Twenty, thirty percent?"

"Zero percent tax? Shoes, too?" Mentally she started doing the math, and although math wasn't her best subject—English always had been—she knew the fast-track to calculating sales tax. On a hundred dollar pair of shoes—

—no, she wasn't going to be sidetracked, not even by the siren's call of shopping. "We need to discuss this," she stated firmly.

"Discuss what?"

"This," she answered, shooting him a meaningful look.

"Another ambiguous pronoun. And you call yourself a writer?"

"I'm being serious."

He sighed, stared, and then sighed again. "What are you afraid of?"

She looked around the room. The dog, the coffee-maker, the little bank and insurance magnets on the refrigerator. Everything here was designed for long-term usage. No fast food, no disposable anything. This wasn't where she belonged.

"Sam, you're running for Congress. Congress. This isn't the town council. What about all those little old ladies in Hackensack, who are shocked, *shocked* that you're shacking up with some sleazy smut-writer. There is no happy ending. One day you'll wake up and go for some blond Sunday school teacher, and imagine all the cute tow-headed boys that the two of you could have together, and then you'll look at me, my nondescript dark hair, my sex blog which uses words like penis and clit on a regular basis, and you say 'I can't do this.' And then where will I be, Sam? Left out on the street without a toothbrush, that's where. I need to go back to my apartment. I don't like relationships. I don't mind the sex, but anything more is setting me up to get hurt."

"You've had relationships before."

"With jerks, yes. It's an automatic safety, sort of like playing Monopoly with a kid. You go in, start the game, and you know you're going to lose, so it doesn't matter. Being with you isn't playing Monopoly, Sam. It's not a game. It's the big leagues. And if I'm stepping into the big leagues, I can't do it knowing I'll end up being hurt."

"I won't hurt you, Mercedes."

"There's not a guarantee with this sort of thing."

"This sort of thing? You mean a relationship?"

"We're not in a relationship," she corrected him. "We're having wild, passionate sex."

"I'm sorry. If we're talking about toothbrushes, we're in a relationship. Do you mind cooking tomorrow? I eventually want to try that ziti."

"Sure."

"See, you're going to cook. We're in a relationship."

"That doesn't count."

"You cook for everyone you have wild, passionate sex with?"

"No."

He gave her a smug smile.

"I can't argue with you, Sam. You're a professional. You get people to say the wrong things all the time. You can't count my misstatements against me."

"I don't want to argue, Mercedes. I like being with you, no, I love being with you. I want to have wild, passionate sex with you. I want talk-time with you. I want to understand your belief system, if you have a belief system, and if you don't it's okay. I like knowing you're there to talk to. It's very strange, but I didn't recognize that I was lonely until now. Not that Max is chopped liver, and speaking of Max—look, even Max is already attached. Are you going to break my dog's heart?"

At the sound of his name, Max looked up, gazed at her with big puppy-dog eyes, and Mercedes didn't want to see that bright light where people never returned. She didn't want refrigerator magnets, or toothbrushes, or casserole dishes full of ziti, or puppy-dog eyes, or the man who made her want every single one of those things. Those things terrified her more than airplane crashes, terrorism, and giant man-eating sharks combined.

"Sam."

He pointed to Max. "Look at that face. How can you deny that face?"

"I'm scared."

"I know. Stay here. Stay with me. I'm not your father, Mercedes. Sometimes you have to trust."

Trust. Now there was a four-letter word. Men weren't designed for trust, they were designed for other four-letter words. "We're going to see Tony tonight?" she asked, deciding to change the subject to something less emotionally upheavalish.

"Just at a bar. No pressure. Very casual. You don't have to take your toothbrush. But maybe you can give him some pointers on relationships."

Mercedes glared.

"You think anyone will notice you?" she asked.

"No, people don't notice me, it won't be a problem."

"Sam, be serious."

"I am."

"What about the reporters?"

"They dog me at the studio, at the talks, but I don't think Sam Porter going to a bar will make CNN."

Mercedes crossed her arms across her chest. "I don't know."

"Tony needs you," he said.

"Fine."

"So, about this story you wrote today. The housewife. Alone. The plumber who comes to fix the showerhead.

For the record, I'd feel a whole lot more secure in this thing that isn't a relationship, this wild, passionate sex, not-a-relationship-thing, if you didn't indulge in sexual fantasies that involved my father."

"Fiction. Hello?"

"Normally I'd buy that line, but you wrote about me, and that was fiction, and yet not. So I know there's a gray area."

"Your father is not in the gray area, Sam. You're the only one in the gray area."

"But why a plumber then? Why not, let's say, a pizza delivery boy?"

"Have you ever seen a pizza delivery boy? They're always scrawny and skinny, and I'm sorry, my imagination doesn't work that hard."

"But plumbers are sexy?"

"Oh, yeah, much more so than pizza delivery boys."

"My father is a plumber, Mercedes. He's been a plumber for over fifty years. You're freaking me out."

"This is not *The Graduate,* Sam. Swear."

"Okay," he said, doubt in his voice.

"If it will make you feel better, no more plumbers. Maybe painters next time."

"Painters would be okay. I'd feel much better about that. You really told my Dad that you're my interior decorator?"

"What was I supposed to tell him?"

He pushed a hand through his hair. "Fine. Let's go, before you decide to decorate the house in pink."

THEY MET TONY AT A SPORTS bar in Jersey. An old dive with a crowd of regulars who were more interested in the basketball game than a Congressional candidate. They found a booth in the corner, and Sam took over the introductions before Mercedes could step in. "Tony, this is Mercedes. Mercedes is the—" Sam stopped in mid-sentence, his tongue wrapped around the words he was going to say. *Woman I'm going to marry.* "—my girlfriend," he corrected smoothly. "If she tells you anything else, it's a lie."

Mercedes looked peeved. "I wasn't going to lie."

Tony studied her, rubbing his jaw. "You look familiar. Have we met before?"

Sam knew where this awkward moment was going. And he knew it was something he would have to learn to live with—starting now. "She's been on the show."

"Ah…." Tony started, before comprehension dawned. "Oh. The writer."

"Yes, I'm the writer," said Mercedes smiling tightly.

Tony looked at Sam, and gave him a thumbs up.

Sam rolled his eyes.

"How are you doing?" Mercedes asked Tony, neatly dodging any more probing questions. Sam shot her a look of gratitude.

"Good. You're the one who wrote my profile, aren't you?"

She nodded.

Tony shook his head in amazement. "You wouldn't believe. Females are interested in me."

"So you've been out on some dates?" asked Sam.

"No. I haven't responded back to anyone. I don't know what to say, what to do. And what if they don't like me? I printed some of the e-mails out, maybe you can help?"

Mercedes patted Tony on the back. "And of course we will. Pick one out of the pile that you like."

Tony pulled out a sheet of paper. "She's in her mid-forties, has two kids, and is looking for a good time only."

Mercedes tapped a finger against her cheek, the wheels turning in her head. "Okay, here's the real deal. She's telling you that she doesn't want a relationship because she's been burned before. Older, got two kids, the first husband, or father of her kids was probably a total jerk, and she's afraid that you're a jerk, too. However, she's hoping against hope that you're not a jerk, because actually she really wants the whole enchilada. But she's got a lot of baggage with her. She has a ready-made family. That's a tough selling point for a lot of men. Are you prepared for a ready-made family, Tony?"

Tony laughed.

"Then you need to walk away. You've got to put her needs before yours, and if she's going to get hurt, you don't even venture into the woods. Got it?"

"But she seems nice, and I wouldn't want to hurt her."

"Aha! Emotional trap number one. The pity-relationship. Don't go there, Tony."

Tony looked at Sam. "You think?"

"She's the expert," he said, with a pointed stare at Mercedes.

She glared back.

Tony drew a red X through the paper.

"Next one?"

"This one is thirty-two years old, never married, is worried she won't ever find her Prince Charming. Those are the words she used, 'Prince Charming,' can you believe it? And she's attractive, likes jazz, and wine—"

"Whoa," interrupted Sam. "Jazz and wine? Tony, do you think you can do jazz and wine? Don't you think you should be yourself?"

"But what if I like jazz and wine?"

"Do you?"

"No."

"See. You have to know what you want. You have to know yourself. You have to think, 'Okay, this is what I like and if it's what I like, then that's what it's going to be.'"

Mercedes made a face. "That doesn't even make sense, Sam."

"It did to me. Tony needs to know his own mind, and have faith in his own decisions, and not second-guess himself. I mean, come on. Jazz and wine? Jazz, okay. Wine, okay. But both? Together? He'd be comatose in two days."

"But what if he hadn't tried jazz, or he hadn't tried wine. What if he tries it, and he likes it, but if he hadn't tried it, then he would have never known."

"I hate jazz," said Tony. "Wine's okay, but I want it with food. If I'm going to sit alone and drink, I want beer."

Mercedes heaved a sigh. "Fine. No jazz or wine. She's probably a supermodel or something."

"No, I've seen her picture."

"Let's move on," said Mercedes.

"Next up is a temp worker. She's young. New to the city, and is looking for someone who can show her around. She's not sure if she wants a relationship or not, but thinks if it works out, then it should."

"There," said Sam. "You should write her back. She's sensible. Not fixated on one thing or another, but open to options and opportunities, since no one knows when options and opportunities might come up."

"I think she sounds flighty and unreliable," answered Mercedes, shaking her head. "She's too young to know what she wants. She moved to New York to make her way in the world, so she's ambitious, but she's going to be shallow and have her head turned by the first hunky guy that comes along."

Tony frowned. "I didn't see that in what she said. Did you see that?"

Mercedes nodded. "Oh, yeah, but you have to know how to read between the lines. It's there. Young. Flighty. Unreliable. Happens all the time."

"Not to disagree, but to disagree, I don't think you should slap all young adults with a label of flighty and unreliable. I know some young people who are responsible and reliable."

Mercedes looked at him skeptically. "I am not responsible."

Sam coughed. "Actually, I was speaking of my stage manager, Kristin. She's young, but she's very reliable. She's usually at the studio before me, and completely un-flighty."

"You think I'm flighty and irresponsible?"

"I think you just said you weren't responsible."

"You think I'm not responsible?"

"I didn't say that. You said that."

"I'm responsible. I'm as responsible as the next person."

"I know you're responsible. You're not flighty and you're pretty reliable."

"You don't think I'm reliable?"

"I think you're reliable," said Tony. "I mean, you

were five minutes late, but that could be because of traffic, and I don't think people should be labeled as unreliable because a deer hurtles through someone's car on the Palisades."

"There wasn't traffic, or a deer. We were late because of Sam."

"Now wait a minute. You started that discussion, not me."

"But you wanted to finish it."

"Well, yes, I did. We couldn't just leave in the middle of a discussion."

Tony's eyes got big. "You guys were having a fight?"

"It was a discussion, not a fight," said Mercedes.

"I wasn't fighting. You were fighting," answered Sam, because he didn't fight. He argued for a living, and he knew about fights, and they hadn't been having one.

"No," snapped Mercedes. "I was discussing. Did I raise my voice? I don't think so."

"But you were disagreeing," Sam pointed out.

"There can be disagreement in discussions. It doesn't have to be a fight."

"A discussion with disagreement is a debate."

"All right then. It was a debate."

"You guys were having a debate?" asked Tony.

"Debates are allowed," Mercedes replied, giving Tony a motherly smile.

And right then, Sam knew.

He loved Mercedes.

There, he admitted it.

He loved her vulnerability, he loved her strength. He loved her ability to put everything out on the table and not worry about it.

He loved her courage, he loved her mind, he loved her body.

Sam had always had an optimistic streak in him, and he wanted to believe that he could work out his relationship with Mercedes, convince her they had a future together, and yeah, win a House seat, too.

Maybe he couldn't have all of those things, but he would give up a seat in Congress before he was going to give up her.

She glanced over, saw him watching, and he smiled.

Tony looked at the paper and scratched his head. "So what's the verdict on young and flighty?"

"No," voted Mercedes.

"Yes," voted Sam.

They continued through the choices for Tony, and finally, the selection had been pared down to a mere five, but Tony still seemed worried.

Tony stared into his beer. "I haven't been out on a date in years," he admitted.

"Don't worry. If it's meant to be, it'll be," said Sam.

"I was with my wife for seventeen years. I thought that was meant to be."

Mercedes smiled at Tony as if the world was going to be okay, as if happy endings were possible and Sam felt his heart squeeze tightly. "You have to try. If you love her, you have to try. If she loves you, really loves you, she's going to try." Mercedes looked at Sam, her eyes sparkling.

Then her lips curved up in a smile, and Sam knew that Mercedes was going to try.

THE NEXT MORNING, SAM MET Martin at the Four Seasons for breakfast. It was a room where movers and shakers congregated, so people knew they were movers and shakers. Sam saw some heads turn as he walked in. Martin had set up this on purpose.

Always needing to spin the appearance.

Sam shook his hand, and they sat down for business. This time, Sam was ready.

"I've listed my core principles. They won't change. You can spin them however you want."

Martin scanned the list. "What's the funding for the arts?"

"I think schools need money for music and art education. I think math and science are still a priority, but they're axing school arts programs all over the state."

"But you're campaigning on lower property taxes."

"That, too."

"You can't have it all, Sam."

"I refuse to believe there's not a way."

"Trust me, you can't put this in a campaign speech."

"Okay," answered Sam, making a mental note to put it into a campaign speech. Possibly tomorrow.

"You saw the papers on Congressman Barnard today? Those promises he made two years ago are just starting to blow up in their faces."

"Barnard is a wuss. No big loss."

"Their loss is our gain." Martin handed him some papers.

"Here's what we've set up for the next two weeks. We'll start easy, hit the northern part of the state first. You'll get good exposure. After that, we'll move further south. It's less friendly territory for you, but I think with a few good quotes in the paper and some cheesy press shots, we can turn some heads. There's a fund-raiser next weekend, and I've given you some bios of the people you want to be nice to. These people will fund your campaign if you let them, and I'm hoping we let them. Any questions?"

Sam took the papers from Martin, and tucked them away. "No."

Martin wore a congenial smile, but his eyes were hard, appraising. "You've been very quiet. Anything I need to know? I'm in this to win, Sam, and I don't like surprises."

Sam met his eyes evenly. "I haven't done anything for you to worry about, but I like my life, Martin, and if people are starting to comb through my garbage, I'm out."

"Nah. Not for a seat in the House."

"Okay. I'll see you at the fund-raiser."

TRIDENT WAS A HUGE, cavernous club on the Lower East Side. An old warehouse building with a tin roof and graffiti covered walls, but what it lacked in exterior design, it more than made up for in post-Apocalyptic style. Black and white videos played on the walls, and if a man looked closely, he would be shocked to realize that the videos were basically soft-porn. Skin flashed, but the images moved so quickly that a man wasn't exactly sure what he was watching, but he kept looking, just to figure it out.

Sam shook his head, trying not to get turned on.

Interspersed were videos from the club floor, people trying to outshock each other to get their faces and bodies on the wall.

It was hedonistic, it was sexy.

Okay, he was getting turned on. Some things a man couldn't fight.

Sam was going to have to kill Franco for this. Sam

looked around, seeing everything that was wrong with America while Tony watched the surroundings with the look of a soldier in the demilitarized zone.

Everywhere there was something to see, something to shock. The women were all young. Way too young, and Sam felt the beginnings of a true midlife crisis approaching. He'd find Mercedes and they'd go someplace simpler, someplace where people could hear.

That was the moment when he spotted her and his throat closed up on him.

Holy moley.

The black leather dress fit her like a glove, a very tight, hand-crafted glove that helplessly maneuvered on every curve. A zipper ran the length of her, from the neck to the top of her thighs, and the zipper was undone about halfway between her breasts.

It was nothing overtly sordid, but a man looked and got ideas. Or at least Sam did.

"Hiya, Sam," she said, coming up, just like an old friend. He hated the pretense, hated the idea that he couldn't just take her hand, kiss her properly, or slip the zipper down just another half an inch, but no matter what he wanted, he knew it was a bad idea.

"This wasn't what I was expecting. We should go somewhere…less."

She laughed then. "More is good, Sam. Remember why you're here," she reminded him, with a meaningful glance in Tony's direction. And she was right, Tony was watching the people on the dance floor, watching the videos on the wall, watching Mercedes with avid, avid interest.

Sam had the strong desire to jab Tony in the ribs,

possibly hard enough to shove his eyes back into their sockets, but she would know, and get upset because he wasn't a "modern man," so he kept his hands to himself, hoping Tony would keep his hands to himself, too.

While he watched, she led his friend out onto the floor until they were swallowed up in a million throbbing people, engaged in an overt mating ritual that had lost any hint of subtlety.

Mercedes wasn't dancing with Tony, more dancing around him, dancing through the crowd, her body beating in time to the heavy bass rhythm on the floor. She was completely uninhibited, twisting and writhing. When she saw someone she wanted to include in their circle, she moved around them, through them, until the circle enlarged.

Tony's dance moves were a little outdated, but Mercedes was a good sport and didn't mind at all. She would mimic whatever he was doing, and somehow, when she did it, it didn't look outdated, it looked graceful and seductive. Tony, bless his heart, was having the time of his life.

And that was the purpose of this mind-altering exercise, Sam kept telling himself. He was a good friend. A great friend, he corrected himself. He was the *Best. Friend. Ever.* But Sam's eyes kept on tracking back to Mercedes, who whirled like a dervish on the floor.

"Sam!"

He blinked at the sound of his name, one hundred percent certain that no one in the eighteen to thirty-four age group would recognize him. Someone slapped a hand on his back, and he turned to see Franco and a woman—most likely the girlfriend. "Franco?"

"Look at you! I didn't think you'd actually come here, being a candidate and all. It's great, isn't it?"

"Marvelous," drawled Sam.

"Where's Tony?"

Sam pointed to the movie on the wall that showed Mercedes still dancing in rings around Tony. "I thought you were cooking tonight."

"I knew this would be more fun. I wanted to see you with your face all scrunched up, trying to keep yourself calm and collected when faced with all this healthy human sexuality."

"Oh, get over yourself," muttered Sam.

"Mandy, this mellow example of wasted manhood is Sam Porter."

"Hiya! You're the TV guy?" she asked.

"Sometimes," he yelled back.

Right then, Tony and Mercedes came back. Tony's face was flushed with excitement and sweat. If Sam were a good friend, he'd tell Tony that he was too old for this nonsense. Instead, Sam kept his mouth shut.

"Franco, Mandy, this is Mercedes. And Tony."

"Nice to meet you," said Mercedes. "I'm here with some friends of mine, they're—" she pointed across the room "—on the far side, and then I took pity on *these* guys, because they didn't know anybody."

Sam rubbed his eyes. "Mercedes. It's okay."

She looked at Sam, looked at Franco, and then stuck out a hand to Mandy. "Hi, Mandy. How're you? You look like you could use a drink. Can you use a drink? I know that I could use a drink. Let's go get a drink, if that's okay?"

She grabbed Mandy's arm and led her toward the bar.

"Is she the hired gun?" asked Franco.

"Nah. She's a friend."

Franco leered. "You've got good taste in friends, Sam. An ever-expanding taste in friends. I approve. She's a lot better than the last blonde you dated. Does she know where China is on a map?"

"Certainly. I think. I'm sure she does. She's very bright."

Then Franco snapped his fingers. "That's the writer."

"What writer?" asked Sam, pretending ignorance, which was not something he normally pretended, but right now ignorant seemed the best way to be.

"The sex books."

"She writes fiction, yes. I wouldn't call them sex books, though."

"They're full of sex?"

"Yes."

Franco stayed silent.

"Yes, she writes the sex books," admitted Sam.

"Does Charlie know about this?"

"He knows what she writes."

"No, does he know that you're nailing her?"

"My private life stays private, Franco."

Franco flagged down a waiter and ordered Sam a drink, a stiff whiskey and water. "You're going to need it."

MERCEDES WAS HAVING AN amazing time. She liked clubs, she loved people, and she got a chance to help out one of Sam's friends. It was a win-win-win. Tony was doing better. She'd worked to pull him out of his shell, although Sam wasn't helping much. He stood, stared, his face immobile.

She went up to him, tugged on his shirt—the black one she picked out for him, she was pleased to note.

"If you're not careful, people will think you're a prude."

"I am a prude. You should know that about me."

"You can't do bondage and still be a prude."

His eyes got bigger. "I thought you didn't want to talk about that."

"Nobody can hear. And that's around your dad. Family is different. You should dance," she told him, crooking a finger in invitation.

"Don't make me dance."

"Why?"

"I'm a mature, intelligent human being, set apart from the animals by my ability to choose not to make a fool of myself in public."

"You should dance," she said, pulling his hand.

"You're not listening to me, you're just using that wicked mind-control look in your eyes to make me think that I could never make a fool out of myself."

"You could never make a fool out of yourself," she said, pulling him farther into the crowd, where he had to either move or be trampled.

And then he was dancing with her, watching her with hungry eyes as their bodies moved in perfect sync.

"This is not the behavior of a mature, intelligent human being. I look just as bad as Tony."

"You're not doing bad. For an old man," she teased.

He caught her close against him, all that merciless, hard muscle pressed against her, breast to chest, thigh to the hard, thick, bulge that made her want to sink against him more. Her sex throbbed in time to the music, pulsing with a heavy beat of its own. Each time his hips moved against hers, she closed her eyes, her mind escaping to a place far away from the dance floor, far away from the public eye.

The public eye. She groaned in frustration. They were dancing closer than they should be. People might think this was taking compassionate conservatism a bit far.

She spun around him, putting some distance between them, but her hands slipped lightning-fast into places they shouldn't be slipping to in public.

He caught her back, their hips locked together, and she didn't fight. It felt too good. Right now her body was in control, not her mind. "I like the dress," he whispered in her ear.

She reached in between them, and pulled the zipper down an inch lower. "It's versatile."

"We'll talk about it later," he said, a warning in his voice. His body moved away from hers, and she felt the loss instantly, but he had done the right thing, damn him.

"See, you're not a prude," she said, sexual frustration coloring her voice, and not in a nice way, either.

"Oh come on, Mercedes. This is all commercialized sexuality."

"So?"

He brushed back the hair from her face, his thumb lingering. "You better rescue Tony, I think he's getting lost again."

Sam was right. Tony was hovering closer and closer to the edge of the wall, nursing a drink in his hand. There was a lot here to overwhelm someone. The crowd of people, faceless, and nameless, the flash of the lights that matched the beat of the music. Everyone was here for one purpose. To meet someone for tonight. Not tomorrow, but only tonight.

Mercedes brought Tony onto the dance floor, searching out the women in the club to find his perfect match. It wouldn't be easy because Tony was too sensitive for most of the barracudas here. They would chew him up and spit him out, but Mercedes was on a mission. A mission for Sam.

Her first candidate, Dora, was too shy. Mercedes knew it, knew that Tony and Dora would never speak at all, merely avoid glances all night. The next girl was Brittany, who was more outgoing, but she had a hard edge to her, so Mercedes shook her off. The last lady was Sylvia. Sylvia was a little older, more a librarian type, but the fact that she'd come to Trident with some of her friends indicated cajones of a non-librarian level. Mercedes approved.

"Want to meet a nice guy tonight? Somebody who will actually call you and ask you out on dates, probably even spring for dinner?"

Sylvia looked at her strangely, but nodded.

"Come with me," said Mercedes, leading Sylvia to Tony, performing introductions, and hoping that nature would work its wayward course. Then she looked at Sam expectantly. "Problem solved."

"Just like that?"

"Of course."

"Are you hungry?"

"No."

"Humor me. Why don't we take Tony—"

"—and Sylvia—"

"—and Sylvia, and find someplace to talk. This has

been a good first step, but I think we should regress to something less intimidating."

"For him or for you?"

"Him."

Because she was so proud of Sam for actually deigning to dance with her, she chose not to argue. "Fine."

However, they did argue about where to go next. Mercedes wanted burgers from the Shake Shack and Sam wanted someplace more comfortable, so they finally ended up at a Starbucks in Soho, settled around a tiny table in the corner.

Sylvia and Tony were still a little bit embarrassed, and Mercedes did her best to keep the conversation flowing, but it wasn't easy.

"Sylvia, where did you say you worked?"

"I didn't."

"So, where do you work?" asked Mercedes patiently.

"I can't say."

"As in, I don't want you to know, or as in 'I work for the CIA'?"

Sylvia scrunched up her brows. "I work for the CIA."

Sam tried not to snicker. "Nice deduction, Sherlock."

However, Tony looked impressed. "The CIA?"

"I'm only a secretary," she added apologetically, sipping at her coffee.

"But a secretary is a really great thing. I mean, you see all those secrets, and hear all that spy-stuff, and I know the CIA is a much smarter place than they talk about in the press. Right, Sam?"

At the mention of Sam's name, Sylvia's eyes widened. "You're Sam Porter! Oh my God. My boss hates you."

"Sorry to hear that, ma'am," he said, and Mercedes noticed the change in his voice. He'd changed from casual man-about-town to aw-shucks midwestern boy without taking so much as a breath. Nice job for a man born in Jersey.

Sylvia blushed bright red, and Tony covered her hand. "It's okay. A lot of people hate Sam. He gets death threats on a daily basis."

"You do?" gasped Mercedes.

Sam gave Tony a warning glance. "Not daily, but I have some enemies. Apparently in the CIA."

Sylvia's face returned to its normal shade of pale. "I shouldn't have said anything. I caught your show a couple of times, but I like the silver-haired guy better."

"Sam's much more distinguished looking. He's like the voice of reason," said Mercedes, deciding that someone needed to take up for the underdog here.

Tony laughed at that. "Sam's the voice of reason unless you got on the wrong side of his opinion. Then he becomes the voice of stubbornness."

"There's nothing wrong with knowing your own mind," argued Mercedes.

Sam looked at her, the devil in his eyes. "I can argue my own defense."

"Not now, honey. You sit back and listen."

Even Sylvia laughed then. The conversation slid all over the place, and it was close to midnight when Sam excused himself.

Mercedes watched him walking toward the facilities, just like any ordinary American, and her heart gave a stutter. This was her guy. Her guy.

She caught up to him, inching a little too close for comfort.

Noticing her (not that she was exactly subtle), he asked, "You headed for the facilities, too, or something else?"

"Just wanted to say hello."

His gaze dropped from her face, lower, lingering somewhere in the valley of her cleavage. "I do love that dress."

"I thought I'd point out a dark corner over there, where a person of a devious nature might cop a feel, sneak a peak, steal a kiss, or all of the above."

He pulled her behind the dark space where the boxes were stored, bringing her to him, his mouth coming down over hers. She didn't notice the zipper sliding down, only the cool breeze hitting bare flesh. He continued to kiss her, his desire apparent in his tongue, in the thick bulge that pressed between her thighs, and then his hands were beneath the material, inside, cupping her breasts, freeing them.

Such marvelous hands, such talented fingers. She stood on her toes, trying to shift even closer, when she heard him swear. His mouth lifted from hers, her dress zipped tightly shut, and the rest of her was throbbing like a mother.

"That wasn't fair," she protested.

"We have company," he whispered, and there was a sound from nearby. An older woman in party clothes held up her cell phone camera and snapped a picture.

It took a second for Mercedes to process the ramifications of the situation. Governments had been brought down for less.

Sam held up a hand, blocking the woman from them, and tried to push his way out, but this was the thing she had feared most.

Mercedes took a step away from Sam, her eyes wide and alarmed. "Oh, my God! You're not Phil! Who are you?"

The woman looked at Mercedes in confusion. "I thought you were his date?"

Sam started to speak and Mercedes jammed her heel on his foot. Hard. "I'm with Phil, not this guy." She gave Sam a hard once-over, squinting in the low light. "You look like Phil, but not quite. I think he's taller."

She turned to the woman. "Don't you think Phil is taller?"

The woman looked at her in confusion. "I don't know how tall Phil is. This is Sam Porter. The talk show host."

Mercedes's jaw dropped. "You're on TV? Oh. My. God. I can't believe it! I was kissing a TV star. Lady, can I see that picture, not that I can show Phil or anything. He'll get like totally P.O.ed and you don't want to be around Phil when he's P.O.ed." She held out her hand, and the woman handed her the camera.

"How can I view the picture?" she asked, and the woman pressed a button for her.

"Oh!" Mercedes made an approving sound. "Would you look at that?" She grinned at Sam. "You're almost as cute as Phil." Then she slid her fingers across the phone, hitting the delete option, and then hitting another button to confirm.

"There!" Mercedes said, and handed the phone back to the woman. "I think those phones are so cool, taking pictures with a telephone? Can you imagine? I'm just a big dork when it comes to technology. Listen, I can hear Phil calling my name. Toodles." She waved at Sam. "Mr. TV Star, it was great to meet you, and I hope you never have to meet Phil. He will so jump all over that really tight ass of yours. He's very possessive, my Phil."

Then she lifted her coat from the chair, and sashayed out of the Starbucks, leaving Tony, Sylvia and Sam Porter far behind.

No, Mercedes had done enough damage for tonight.

HER CELL PHONE RANG TWICE before she shut it off. She knew it was Sam, but she wasn't ready to talk to him. What could Mercedes say? She could quit her writing and walk away from her career, which would be a lot easier if her book wasn't currently out in every bookstore in America—going into a second printing.

Tonight she should have known better. Stupidly, she had forgotten they lived in a world where cameras lurked around every corner, and a moment's indiscretion could turn up on the Internet. Majorly stupid, because she wrote about those indiscretions in her blog. Good one, Mercedes. Chalk one up in the idiot column.

She walked up Broadway, and then down Houston, past the Saturday night crowds, past the couples, past the packs of smokers that congregated outside the club doors. The fall air was cold on her legs and she was grateful for the warmth of her dress, but it didn't help the cold that was inside her. All those sweet ideas of permanence and security were currently out the window.

She walked past the newspaper kiosk, past the Number One Chinese restaurant. She had known all along that they couldn't be together. She had tried to tell him, but he wouldn't listen. Maybe now he would listen. Maybe now he would leave her. The hurt pierced through the cold, pierced through the walls she'd built to protect herself. She didn't want to hurt.

Outside her building, her heel got caught in one of the steam grates, and she pulled, trying to get it free. No matter how hard she tried, it was stuck. Hell.

She jerked again, leaving one broken heel stuck in the sidewalk. She took off the shoe and threw it in the street.

Damn Choos.

Damn. Damn. Damn.

Why had she thought this could work? It would never work. Sam was honorable, upstanding, and he didn't need someone who wrecked everything she touched.

Mercedes trampled up the four flights of stairs, one heel, one bare foot. When she got to her door, Sam was there. Waiting.

14

"WHY ARE YOU HERE?"

"Open the door, Mercedes. Let's not talk in the hall. It's late."

She didn't want to let him inside. She wasn't strong enough to resist him. She wasn't one of his politico guests, she was just the woman who loved him.

And because of that, she unlocked the door, and he followed her inside.

He didn't look angry, didn't look mad, he took her in his arms, held her close, so tightly, like he would never leave her.

Mercedes began to cry. She wasn't an elegant crier, it was dramatic, loud and never pretty.

Sam didn't seem to mind. He stood, stroking her hair, making it harder and harder for her to do the right thing.

"I love you, Mercedes."

Oh, God. That was below the belt, dirty pool and a personal foul. It only made her cry harder.

"I think I knew a year ago. I just looked at you, looked in your eyes and fell. I didn't want to. You were trouble. I knew it, and I spent the last year trying to do my job, live my life, forgetting about you. You know how stubborn I am. But I couldn't forget. You were always there. Always in my head. It took me over a year to come up with a legitimate excuse to see you again. And the first shot I had, I took it. I thought we'd sleep together, and that'd be the end of it. But it was the start of it, not the end. I'd wake up thinking about you, wondering what you would say, wondering which smile you were wearing. You have at least three that I know of. The plain-jane, life is great smile. The snarky little Miss Brooks smile, and then there's the last smile. The one you don't flash very often, but God, when you do… Every neuron in my brain lights up like a pinball machine on tilt. I stumble over my words, and that from a man who gets paid a lot of money never to stumble over words. I have that picture stuck in my head forever. I know it's fast, I know it doesn't make sense, I don't have any facts to back it up, but I've accepted it. Love isn't logical."

"Sam, we'll get caught. And next time, there won't be a way out."

"Then I'm not in the election. I don't like people intruding in my private life. I don't like flashbulbs going off in my face. I don't want to end up in the tabloids. If I don't run, that problem is solved."

"That's not an option."

"It is for me."

"What about the show?"

"The show will be fine. I'll be fine. We'll be fine."

She cushioned her head on his chest, listening to the quiet thud of his heart, feeling so safe, so secure, but Sam Porter couldn't fix everything, and she knew what was going to happen if they stayed like this. His career would be ruined. His image would be shattered, and there would be no one to blame but her.

All through the night she let him love her, let him whisper in her ear, let him hold her, but this time Mercedes held back a small piece of herself.

It was time to rebuild the walls around her heart.

AN AFTERNOON OF WORKING for her sister-in-law Sheldon should have been exactly what Mercedes needed. Work was a chance to keep her mind off other things, namely her relationship with Sam. The Battery Park apartment Sheldon and Jeff shared had been transformed into a full-fledged activity zone. Sheldon's new project to bring music to inner-city kids was up and running. There was a table with office supplies and a fax spewing pages. Stacks of paper and envelopes were everywhere, and judging by the size of her pupils, Sheldon looked to be on her fifth cup of coffee.

Mercedes studied the place in awe. "Wow. I have to say, that for a pair of slackers, this puts Jamie and Andrew to shame."

Sheldon just looked nervous. "There's so much to do. You wouldn't believe how much work is involved in actual work."

Jeff put an arm around his wife. "Spoken like a princess who's never lifted a finger."

Mercedes rubbed her hands together, forcing a smile. "Ah. All this love, it makes my heart go pitter-patter. So what am I supposed to do?"

"Okay, slave, we'll start you with easy stuff. Check over these press releases and see if you find any glaring typos."

"Check check. I can do that." Mercedes took the pieces of paper and collapsed on the couch to read.

"So when are we going to hear?" asked Sheldon.

"Hear what? Nothing to hear. I hear nothing."

"You haven't been home much, Mercedes."

"Busy, this and that."

"Yeah?"

"Yup. Lots of this. Lots of that."

"What's his name?"

"He has no name. There is no him. I've just been doing a lot of work for the book."

"Right," said Jeff skeptically.

Sheldon wasn't letting her off the hook so easily. "So if a certain someone happened to mention to me that they had seen you in the company of a certain well-known political candidate at a certain club last night, that'd be wrong. Right?"

Mercedes nodded, keeping her head down. "Right. That's definitely wrong."

"And if that someone also mentioned the exact leather dress that I remember buying with you down in the West Village, well, they'd be wrong again. Right?"

"Right. That's definitely wrong."

"Oh, when are you going to stop it, Mercedes? Everybody in the family knows."

Mercedes didn't want this, she wasn't ready to have this discussion, especially when there probably wouldn't be anything to discuss. "Can you leave me alone?"

Jeff raised an eyebrow, shared a look with Sheldon, and then went back to typing on the computer.

Mercedes edited press releases, stuffed envelopes, and made phone calls. Six hours, and seven paper cuts later, she didn't feel any better, but at least the piles were getting smaller.

Jeff ordered pizza, and while they were eating, Mercedes looked at her sister-in-law with new eyes. "So you're in charge of a concert?"

"Not in charge, exactly. I'm just organizing. It's the first fund-raiser for the foundation. We'll have some local orchestra kids play in the St. James Theater, and charge rich people a total fortune to get in and see it. Raise some awareness. Get some bucks, and hopefully fund a few more orchestra programs for the non-arts schools in the city."

"Ambitious," said Mercedes in between bites.

"Not so much," muttered Sheldon.

"She runs from the 'A' word," whispered Jeff.

"I'm just a schlub," answered Sheldon.

Mercedes smiled, because Sheldon still didn't take teasing well. "Not so much. So, the countdown to the McNamara-Brooks nuptials begins."

"Right now."

"Strippers all ordered for the bachelor party, Jeff?"

"Bite your tongue," snapped Sheldon.

"Well, after the bachelor party that Andrew threw for you…" Mercedes said, trailing off.

"What bachelor party?" asked Sheldon.

"There was no bachelor party, Sheldon."

Mercedes checked her watch. "Oops. Look at the time. Gotta go."

HER NEXT STOP WAS HER mom's house because sometimes there truly was no place like home.

Thea Brooks was an aspiring actress, who had spent

roughly forty years aspiring. However, with Andrew's help, they'd always had a roof over their head, and food on the table, and Mercedes's mother was no closer to her dream than when she started, but she was happy.

She stared at her daughter with that unique mom-sense that mothers had. "What's wrong?"

"Not a lot."

"You wouldn't be here if something wasn't wrong."

"Maybe I just want to see my mother. Did you think about that? Spend some quality mother-daughter time with the woman who spawned me."

Her mother smiled with that "not a chance" look.

"I want to ask you a question," Mercedes stated.

"Shoot."

"You've always gone after your dream, done what you wanted, but say that my father would have stayed with the family. Would you have given it up?"

"I thought this was going to be an easy question. You didn't used to ask hard questions, Mercedes."

"So would you have quit?"

"You're thinking of quitting your writing?"

Mercedes would give up her writing in a second for Sam, but it wouldn't make a difference in the election. It was a grand gesture, but one that was still much too late. "Actually I'm more interested in what happens when someone chooses to give up something for someone else. If you had done it, would you have resented him?"

"With your father, resentment comes easy."

"But what if he wasn't such an s.o.b., and you loved him, really loved him, but you gave up something important. Something big. Wouldn't you be mad—deep down inside?"

"Did he ask me to give it up?"

"No, he didn't want you to give it up, but you opted to do it because you knew it was the only way you could be together."

"I thought this was one question."

"I don't know, Mom. I think it's a whole lifetime of questions, and I'm not sure what the answers are."

"You want to tell me?"

Mercedes looked down at her hands. "I love someone. He loves me. He wants to do something big, important and noble with his life, but if he's with me, he can't. I'm baggage. He wants to give it up, so we can be together, but I think he'll hate me eventually."

"You're not anybody's 'baggage,' Mercedes."

"Trust me when I say this. For him, right at this moment in time, I'm baggage."

"What does your heart tell you to do?"

"Walk away."

"Your heart?"

"I want the best for him. It's a huge thing he's trying to do. It's not just writing, or acting, or something like this. This is big. I think he should have it."

"That's a decision you're going to have to make, little girl. But you're nobody's baggage."

Deep inside, Mercedes suspected her mother was wrong. Twenty-six years ago, Mercedes had been excess baggage, her father had left. Fast forward to the present, it was Mercedes that was going to lose the election for Sam. In her book, that counted for baggage.

Some folks weren't ready for a congressman whose girlfriend wrote about turgid ridges of flesh pumping inside her warm, dewy lips. If she quit her writing, people would dismiss it as a reluctant gesture. It wouldn't matter if they were right or wrong, it would only hurt Sam's career.

If Sam quit the campaign, yeah, they'd be together, but at what cost? New Jersey would have lost the best congressman they'd ever had. And Sam would lose his chance to make a difference. Maybe there'd be later chances, maybe not. There were no easy answers.

Her mother gave her a hug, stuffed a twenty in her pocket, and sent her home. Mercedes arrived to an empty apartment. She flipped on her computer, and went to work. Everything she wrote was crap, mainly because she felt like crap, but she kept plugging away, because there wasn't anything else to do. She watched the sunset over the rusted fire escape, but this time it wasn't paradise. Reality had started to intrude.

SAM'S FUND-RAISER was at the Waldorf, and Tony escorted Mercedes. She hadn't wanted to go, but Sam was being stubborn, and she wasn't up to arguing with Sam when he was stubborn. Besides, she'd lose. He'd look at her with those dreamy green (not hazel) eyes, whisper to her in that husky voice, and her spine would melt to nothing. The rat knew exactly what he was doing.

The dress she wore was long, white, buttoned up to the neck, with flowing sleeves. She'd gone shopping and bought it especially for this occasion. Mercedes called it her angel of mercy dress.

The eighteenth floor had an art deco hall with palm trees filling the corners, and somewhere in the distance, the ghosts of Fred Astaire and Ginger Rogers were tap-dancing across the marble floor. The reception tables were decorated with a tasteful, yet patriotic, red, white and blue. Mercedes walked into the room on Tony's arm, and the first thing she saw was Sam, who took one look at her, and then blinked.

"Halloween coming a little late this year?" he asked.

"You're not supposed to be talking to me."

He shot her a long look. "I'm a politician now. I'm supposed to talk to everybody. You're part of everybody. We get to talk."

"Sam."

"Mercedes."

"No one's going to talk to me?" Tony asked. "I'm the fake-date here, shouldn't someone be talking to me?"

Mercedes patted his hands. "Do you want me to find you a campaign staffer that you can take home for the night? If you'll feed me salacious details, I'll write them up in my blog. Anonymous, of course."

"You do anonymous so well," drawled Sam.

Tony looked hopeful. "There are a lot of women here?"

Sam grinned. "Most of them are gainfully employed, have advanced college degrees, and are in the upper one percent of the tax bracket. It's not a bad place to troll for babes."

Tony looked even more hopeful. "Do you think they'll mind that I'm not of their political persuasion? I could pretend if it'd help me meet somebody."

Mercedes scoffed. "You're willing to jettison your political party affiliation for sex? Amazing the times we're in now, more and more people are voting independent."

Sam shot her a look. "You've been watching CNN again, haven't you?"

"I'm trying to learn your business, that's all."

"I'm much better looking than their anchors."

"I thought you didn't think of yourself as a pretty boy? I thought you wanted to be loved for your mind. Can't live on both sides of that fence, Sam."

Sam sighed. "Tony, can you get us some drinks? I need to talk to one of my constituents. Taxes. They're a killer."

"Sure, I'll get the drinks. Two beers. Mercedes?"

"Wine, please. White."

Tony nodded. "Okay. What do you think about the lady in the red dress. You think she'll talk to me?"

"That's the governor's wife, Tony."

"Oh," he muttered. "I'll just get the drinks, then."

Tony took off, leaving them alone and Sam studied her dress some more. "I gotta say that dress is growing on me. A nice contrast to the leather, but it still works. Kinda nurse/schoolteacher/librarian fantasy all mixed together. I could get you a pair of those secretary glasses, maybe some edible underwear, and we could play later."

"You are *so* not making this easy."

"I'm trying to be charming."

"Charming? You've just sent Tony off like an errand boy. You're not being a good friend."

"Are you kidding? You're his date. I think Tony's the big winner tonight. Of course, if he laid a hand underneath any of that virginal white lace, I'd have to kill him."

"Why are you in such a good mood?"

"Because you're here," he answered simply.

The words touched her more than she wanted, but she understood. "You look spiffy tonight. No plaid. I'm proud."

And he did look good. He'd worn something dressier than the usual sports jacket he wore on the show. The dark suit made his hair shine with sprinkles of gold, and he'd tamed some of the tousles. His tie was the conservative maroon stripe, favored by most of the men in the room. But her gaze kept wandering back to his eyes, which were actually more hazel than green tonight. Those eyes were bright with excitement, and she knew that not all of that was because of her. Sam wanted this, and she knew it. He loved the idea of duty and honor, of thinking for the good of the country.

"I thought you'd approve," he said.

Tony returned, and Sam mingled, but every now and then, he'd look up, see her. Over the course of the evening, Mercedes met tons of New Jersey's political elites. She wanted to tell them she voted for the other guy in the last election, just for shock value, but she kept her mouth shut. This was Sam's night to shine.

And he shone. All the players were there. The fat cats, the bureaucrats, the other politicians, but Sam stood out. He wasn't worried about pleasing the base, or negotiating deals for dollars. He simply wanted to do right by the state of New Jersey.

Mercedes sighed. It was enough to make her change her statehood. She had just taken a sip of champagne, when a man approached. Shorter, a young ambitious type, with stylish horn-rimmed glasses, and dark, gleaming eyes.

"Miss Brooks? We haven't had the pleasure. I'm Martin Darcy, Sam's campaign manager."

She nodded politely. "Ah, yes, the campaign manager. I'm here with Tony, Sam's friend."

"I saw the tape of you on Sam's show a few weeks back," he said, and she realized those dark, gleaming eyes didn't miss a thing.

"Oh, yeah."

"That's one of Sam's better qualities, the ability to listen to both sides, find common ground, and move forward."

Mercedes laughed, a delicate, trilling laugh. "I'm not convinced we found common ground. In fact, I'm almost positive that no ground was common at all. Ever. We ended up on an agreement to disagree. I write sex books. He doesn't approve."

Martin smiled. "He's a real asset to the party this year and it'd be a real disappointment if he lost."

"Oh, Sam's gonna win," said Mercedes.

"I didn't think you were a fan."

Damn. "Oh, I'm not a fan, but the other candidate? He's bathtub-scum. It's actually a lose-lose situation for me, being the loyal liberal that I am. But if I have to choose, if someone chains me down on a rack and forces me to vote, then I suppose I'll hold my nose, and hope against hope—"

"I get it, Miss Brooks."

"Good," she said. If he wanted to play games, then she could play, too. "Ah, yes. And speak of the devil," she said, spying Tony approaching, and taking his arm. "My date. The love of my life." She gave him a warm kiss on the cheek. "Come, darling, let's mingle."

SAM CAUGHT UP WITH HER at the dessert table. "I understand there's a big riot on the roof. I was going up to take a look. You should look, too," he said, putting a hand in the small of Mercedes's back and guiding her down the hallway, through an old storage room, around an air conditioning service corridor, and then pushing through a metal maintenance-type door.

"I don't think we're supposed to go on the roof," she whispered.

"I know for a fact we're not supposed to go on the roof, but I'm an investigative reporter, and sometimes, believe it or not, I actually investigate the facts, rather than just blindly spew them out on my show. Tonight, we're investigating the roof."

"Sam."

"It's true," he answered, leading her up through one narrow flight of stairs, down another service corridor, and then up a narrow flight of stairs.

Finally, success.

The door opened up to New York at night, dressed in her Saturday evening best. St. Patrick's Cathedral was lit up with white spotlights on the gothic towers. The regal structure looked like something out of a medieval fairy-tale. Rockefeller Center was prepping for the weekend crowds, and in the distance, the tiny pinpoints of streetlamps outlined Central Park.

This was the city she loved.

The wind blew around them, but Mercedes didn't really mind the chill. It was so beautiful to watch, so peaceful. So lonely. In New York, it was so easy to feel small, so easy to feel lost.

Mercedes leaned against the ledge, and watched the world, shivering.

Sam came up behind her, strong arms wrapping around her, warming her from the chill, alleviating the loneliness. And who would keep her warm when he was gone? Who would stop the loneliness? There wasn't anyone else.

"You're okay?" he asked. "It's nice, isn't it?"

It was the understatement of the year, but she nodded. "You'll have to go back soon."

"Too soon."

"You're doing very well out there."

"God," he said, his chest rumbling with laughter. "I didn't realize how many people like me."

She turned in his arms, turned away from the city she loved, and looked at him, looked in his eyes, memorizing every detail, the hard line of his jaw, the once-broken nose, the marvelous, expressive eyes that could trap her with a look.

"You're going to win, did you know that?"

"I like to think positively, so yes, I think I'm going to win."

"You'll be a wonderful congressman. And they're going to name elementary schools after you, and maybe build the Sam Porter Parkway."

"I don't think they should call it the Sam Porter Parkway."

"Okay, maybe not. But you're going to do great. You know that, right?" she said, her voice quivering, and she didn't want it to quiver. Not now. This was supposed to be a perfect time. Their perfect time.

"Mercedes?" he asked, his thumb brushing her tears away.

She sniffed and waved her hand in the air. "Sorry. I'm just so happy."

He tucked her head against his chest, rubbing her

back, and once again she was there, leaning against him. It felt so nice. So wonderfully, permanently nice.

"Yeah, I can feel all that happiness radiating from you. I know you hate this, and I'm sorry. We can leave in an hour, I think. Duck out."

"That sounds great," she murmured.

"You sure you're all right?"

"I'm great. I love you, Sam Porter."

She could feel the stillness in him. She hadn't meant to say that, but the words had tripped out.

Gently he grasped her chin, and tilted her mouth for his kiss. Mercedes had never dreamed of magical, starlight nights, and the noble knights who rode on white horses, but he was the stuff that magic was made of. He made her dream. She'd always imagined she was too tough to dream, too tough to love, but now she knew the truth. Love took strength and courage. It was the cowards who were afraid of love. She'd been wrong all along.

She kissed him with all of those dreams, all of that magic, and she hoped he would understand. This night, this kiss, this time, it would be hers, and hers alone.

This time, it was Mercedes who pulled away. "You should get back," she said. When they walked downstairs, her legs were steadier, her back was straighter. She would be fine.

She picked up a glass of champagne, said a quiet goodbye to Tony, and then walked out of the hotel. She hailed a cab back to her apartment, and before she went inside, she threw her cell phone into a passing garbage truck.

She could pack up her things, bunk with her mother for a little, lie low so that Sam couldn't find her.

She would be fine, she didn't have a choice.

15

SAM TRIED TO CALL HER, HE tried going to her apartment. He sent flowers, he sent e-mails, but it was as if Mercedes had disappeared. Her apartment had been vacated, even her agent wouldn't return his calls.

The one bit of hope was the few lines she'd written in her blog.

The nights were unbearably long without him, without his warmth next to her. She'd grown accustomed to the way he held her, the way his body molded to hers. She'd grown accustomed to reaching out in the darkness and finding him there, a brush of the hand to know he was next to her, a bolder touch if she needed something more. She missed the lovemaking in the dark, in the wee hours of the morning, before the sun would come up through the woods. She missed that moment when he would slip inside her, filling a void that was more than physical.

She'd never known how lonely she was before. But now she did, and the pain was even worse.

The headlines in the *Star-Ledger* on Wednesday trumpeted soundbites from Sam's latest campaign speech. He made the nightly news, and had a national television interview. He answered all the questions, smiled when he was told to, but in his heart he had a void that he hadn't even known he'd possessed. It was that warm spot in his heart that Mercedes had claimed for her own.

It took two days for Sam to figure it out. At first, he thought he'd done something wrong, but on Tuesday morning, he met Martin in his office, and Martin looked more pompous than usual. A kingmaker moving his pawns.

"What did you tell her?"

"Who?"

"Mercedes."

"Miss Brooks? Why should I tell her anything?"

"Because everything was fine before the fund-raiser, and after the fund-raiser, everything was not fine."

"Everything was not 'fine' before the fund-raiser, Sam. You were only pretending it was all roses and kittens. You need to learn to take off the Mr. Smith Goes to Washington glasses before you hit DC, or you won't last a week."

"What did you tell her?"

"Actually, I didn't tell her anything. I think she was smart enough to figure it out on her own."

"You're fired, Martin."

"You've got to be kidding. I'm the best. At this late date, you can't get anybody else good enough. Do you want to win this election?"

"Right at the moment, no."

"Good luck, Sam. You're going to need it."

Martin was right.

MERCEDES WENT TO SEE Portia in her midtown office. The agency was a busy place, people cranking six-figure deals over the phone, interns in black, rushing to get signatures for contracts.

Portia was talking on the phone, but she waved Mercedes in.

"Listen, Sal. That's too low. I want the rights to UK, Germany and Eastern Europe. You get the U.S. and Canada.

"No, I'm not letting you have Germany. I've already got an editor over there who's ready to hop all over this. You're not taking my piece of the pie. Got it?

"I mean it, Sal. We get Germany, or the deal's off.

"Talk it over with Mary and get back to me. I'll give you twenty-four hours. The clock is ticking, Sal. Tick. Tick."

She hung up, and looked at Mercedes. "How's my favorite hot novelist? And I mean that in terms of dollars, not editorial content."

Mercedes cracked a smile. "Great."

"You should be on top of the world. Things have really picked up on the sales. I think this demand caught the publisher with their pants down around their ankles. They're going back for a third printing."

"You know, I'm not sure that a third printing is a good idea," answered Mercedes. "I don't know how many people are actually reading it."

"Well, at least an editor at *HIM* is, because there's someone who wants to interview you, get some stories. Evidently you're the quintessential New York success story."

"She's probably following up on the blind item I did on the women's magazine intern who was sleeping with her married boss."

Portia laughed. "You're so cynical, Mercedes. And I thought I was jaded. Ha!"

Mercedes shook her head. She wasn't about to do that to Sam—promote herself in that kind of magazine. They might not be seeing each other, but she'd be loyal. "No, I better not."

Portia's eyes widened behind the glasses. "What? What are you doing to me, doll?"

"Stick with the standard stuff, Portia."

"Like beggars can be choosers? You're sure?"

Mercedes nodded. "Yeah." She rose, ready to leave, ready to go back and work. "Anything else?"

Portia looked at her watch. "I thought we could do lunch."

"Not today. I'm not feeling well. Probably a winter cold coming on."

"Go get some rest then. I'll be in touch."

Mercedes took the subway to her mother's apartment, pondering why the fates had decided to smile upon her now. *Now* she was hitting it big. *Now* she would have great sales, and now she didn't care. The pathway to her happiness lay in Sam, not the *New York Times* bestseller list.

Yeah, big whoop.

She found her mom in her apartment running lines for her next audition. A toothpaste commercial. When her mom saw her, she put down her script.

"More bad news?"

"No. Good stuff."

"Then why do you look like somebody died?

"Nobody died."

Mercedes faked a smile. "I think I'll write for awhile. Can I borrow your bedroom for an hour or so?"

"Sure," her mother replied, and then paused for a minute. "Mercedes, I love you staying here; it's like when you were a kid, but when are you going to go home? You're acting like this is permanent. You don't eat. I see you working in here until early in the morning. And I found two empty boxes of Twinkies in the trashcan, and you don't even like Twinkies. I don't know who did this to you, but if I find out, I'm going to have to—well, kick his ass. Nobody hurts my little girl."

"Mom. I'm fine. Go back to your lines. I'll be out of here soon. I can't go back to my place right now. I let the lease expire. I'll find a new apartment before Andrew's wedding."

Her mother shook her head slowly. "I don't know, Mercedes."

"I've got some work to do."

"Before you do that, can you go down and pick up the mail?"

Mercedes nodded.

As soon as Mercedes was out the door, Thea picked up the phone. "Andrew. This is your mother. You've got to do something."

ON THURSDAY NIGHT, Sam interviewed the superintendent from the Newark school system. He was easier on her than he normally would have been, letting her slide when she glossed over the decrease in test scores. And she'd been thrilled and more than slightly confused when he asked her why they'd been cutting their funding for the arts.

Kristin looked at him in surprise, but he simply shrugged and moved on to the next question.

That night, after the taping was finished, Charlie met him in the bar, and Sam downed a whiskey in one swallow. "How's life as a candidate so far?"

"Sucks."

"Don't worry. It won't get better."

"Maybe I shouldn't be doing this, Charlie."

"What the— Sam. I'm going to have to hit you if you pull out of this now. Look at what's happening around you, in the country, in the world, and then look at your opponent. Tell me, Sam. Who would you want to represent Jersey? Or represent the country? Tell me that, Sam. Give me the facts, here."

"Charlie, this election better not have ruined my life."

"She'll come around."

"What?"

"Mercedes. She'll come around."

"You knew?"

"Hell, yes, Sam. You walked around the studio, smiling, whistling, even starting to call the crew by name. Do you think we're all idiots? We are a news show. It's our job to figure out news."

"She won't talk to me."

"I know. I have days like that, too, but I stop being mad at you."

"I didn't do anything, Charlie. She's just being noble. She doesn't think I can win if I'm with her."

"You might not."

"Then I don't care, but I don't want the press dragging her through the mud because of me."

"God, how did you two ever get together?"

"I don't know," muttered Sam.

"Maybe she's tougher than you think. Maybe you're tougher than you think."

"What's that supposed to mean, Charlie?"

"You figure it out, Sam. Anyway, you have a campaign speech tomorrow night for the top pharma executives in the state. So smile, look pretty, and try to raise millions of dollars for the party."

"I don't look pretty," he yelled, as Charlie slapped a bill on the bar, and then walked out the door.

SAM HAD GIVEN SPEECHES AT benefits before, but never had he felt less like being an entertainer or a campaigner. For once, he wanted to look out over the audience, say "Screw you," and go home. He wanted to be left alone, he wanted to think, but everywhere he turned, people wanted a piece of him. He had always enjoyed his work, but coming into the studio now, pretending to care about trade deficits was the hardest thing he'd ever done. And now, up on stage, talking passionately about problems that he would normally be concerned about, Sam added a new fact to his repertoire. He was a damn good actor. The audience nodded, smiling and clapping as he spoke about the looming issues that faced the country. Inside, Sam only felt numb.

Afterwards, he sat at the table on the dais, ate his rubbery chicken, and listened attentively as Harvey congratulated him on his speech. Over dessert he excused himself because he needed to be alone. All he needed was a few minutes of escape.

He washed his face with cold water, walked out into the hallway, where he saw two men approaching, one familiar.

Being of optimistic nature, Sam's first thoughts were that Mercedes had changed her mind, and sent her brothers to talk for her. But then he took a good look at the cold darkness in both sets of dark eyes. Familiar dark eyes.

Not so good. Par for the course for his life at the moment.

"What do you want?" he asked Jeff Brooks. "Coming to hit me again?"

The older one spoke, his voice tight. "We came to contribute to the campaign, Porter."

"You must be Andrew," said Sam. "I wish we had met under better circumstances." Sam held out a hand, still being of optimistic nature, even in the face of staggering odds, and Mercedes's two really angry older brothers.

Everybody ignored his hand, so Sam dropped it. "Where's Mercedes?" he asked.

Jeff's face closed off. "Leave her alone."

And at that, all the rage that'd been stored up inside Sam came pouring out in a rush. "No. I will never leave her alone, do you understand? Get used to it. I don't know what she's doing right now, I don't even pretend to understand why her mind rolls the way it does, but I will never, *ever* leave her alone. Why the hell are you here?"

"To have a chat," answered Andrew. "To talk about what you did to her."

"What I did to her? She left me, not the other way around. I've tried everything to get her to change her mind. I offered to ditch the campaign. I don't know what else to do."

"You love her?" asked Jeff.

"What? You think I go begging and pleading for the fun of it? I don't think so."

"Do you love her?" repeated Jeff.

"Yeah."

"What are you willing to do for her?" asked Andrew.

"Whatever it takes."

Jeff nodded. "Good. I've got an idea."

AFTER THE BANQUET, JEFF and Andrew went to Andrew's apartment, where Jamie and Sheldon were waiting.

"Did it work?" asked Sheldon.

"Like a charm," replied Jeff with a pleased look on his face.

Sheldon clenched a victory fist. "Yes."

Jamie stood back in awe. "You guys are the most conniving family I have ever met."

"You've got four weeks to change your mind, Jamie," Sheldon reminded her. "After that, you have no choice."

"Don't give her any ideas," Andrew cut in. He looked at Jamie. "She was joking."

Jamie came over, put an arm around his waist. "Four weeks?" she asked, her eyes teasing.

"Not funny."

"You'll get rid of the doves before the wedding?"

"You don't know how hard I worked to get those doves."

"Kill the doves," Jamie insisted.

Andrew raised a brow.

"Not literally," she corrected.

"I suppose you don't like the horse-drawn carriages, either?"

"I have my own ideas," answered Jamie mysteriously.

"What ideas?"

"Ha. It's not so easy when the shoe is on the other foot, is it Mr. I Must Handle Everything?"

Jeff nodded with approval. "Nicely done, Jamie. You got him. I'll tell you more dirt after you're married."

"Don't you dare," snapped Andrew.

"So now we have to sit around and wait?" asked Sheldon.

Jeff frowned. "No. Now's the time when we eat dinner. Some of us are starving."

"Chinese?" asked Andrew.

"You buying?" asked Jeff.

Andrew rolled his eyes. "Yes."

Jeff grinned. "Morton's then. I think steak sounds good." He looked at Andrew's dark face. "To celebrate."

Jamie nudged Andrew in the ribs. "Not a problem."

Jeff smiled happily. "I think you'll fit into the family just fine." He looked at Andrew. "I like her."

16

THE ST. JAMES THEATER WAS one of the grand dames of Broadway. Mercedes wasn't the fan of classical music that Sheldon was, but she supported her family, and it's not as if she had a million other places to be. No, she belonged here at the concert for Sheldon's foundation.

Andrew's box seats were on the first tier, and had a perfect view of the orchestra. Sheldon came out, elegant and gorgeous, and thanked the audience, still nervous. The great velvet curtains lifted, and thirty of New York City's most talented student musicians proceeded to play.

Okay, they were good. Heck, they were great. Mercedes closed her eyes and let the music carry her away to another place.

The kids, and they were kids, played fast songs, slow songs and sad songs. She didn't want sad songs, she wanted the fast ones, and happy ones. And for a while, everything was fine, but then, it got too much for her. Quietly she excused herself, and stood in the hallway outside.

"Hello, Mercedes."

She knew that voice. That beautiful, husky voice. She didn't want this right now. This was Sheldon's night.

"I knew you'd be here. You're a tough lady to find."

"I was staying with my mother." Her eyes wandered

up over his face, because she couldn't resist. It'd been three weeks, but it felt like years.

"You could have at least said goodbye."

"I did, Sam."

"Most people don't assume that 'I love you' is synonymous with goodbye, Mercedes."

"It wouldn't have worked."

"You could have tried."

"No, I couldn't. There was too much at stake."

He swore under his breath, and looked at his watch. Applause sounded from the theater, and Mercedes started to walk back into the box.

"No," he said, and then he caught her in his arms, tipping her towards him, and he was kissing her. It took less than a beat of her heart for her arms to steal up around his neck, as if they belonged there. He pressed her against the wall, crushing her there. All control was gone, and she could feel the hunger inside her, the answering hunger that matched his.

All she could think, all she could feel was here. The lights began to flash in her mind, in her eyes. A prism of colors exploding, blinding her. She worked to see, saw only a myriad of colors, and then she heard the voices.

"Sam Porter?"

"That's the writer!"

She put up a hand to block the lights, and her vision returned. A pack of reporters was jammed in the narrow passageway of the theater.

Not this, not now. Sam put an arm around her, keeping her hidden. He looked at the reporters and spoke. "Listen, guys, I've worked with most of you and I'm asking a favor. I need a few minutes alone. In the morning, you can ask me all the questions you want. On the record."

There was some murmur of disagreement, but Sam knew how to get what he wanted, and he led Mercedes through the crowds of people now streaming from the theater. She and Sam exited through a side door that opened onto the street.

She looked up at Sam, ready to apologize, but he didn't look mad. He put his coat around her, looking remarkably calm.

Calm? Shouldn't he be upset? She was upset. She was furious.

They walked down into the heart of Times Square, past the marquees, past the news crawls, past the five-story advertisements. As soon as they made it to the corner of 47th, she had put two and two together, and smelled a conspiracy. "You set that up," she accused, her voice starting to get a little loud.

"Mercedes, not here."

She put her hands on her hips. "Why not here, Sam? I mean, if you want the entire world to know we're sleeping together, then why not here?"

"Mercedes, we can wait to have this conversation."

"No, we can't. This is what you wanted."

"To be frank, *this* wasn't what I wanted. I had thought we could talk in private because the cameras will always bug me."

"Well, hell, Sam, let's put it up on the marquees. Sam Porter screws erotic writer. I can see the crawl on CNN, now. Your campaign manager will be laughing his ass off."

"You're mad."

"Of course I'm mad. You were supposed to *win.*"

What are you doing?" She couldn't believe this. She hadn't walked away from the best thing in her life, so that he could throw his chances out the window.

He grabbed her arm, fingers tight and painful as they dug into her skin. She glared at him, trying to channel some intelligence into that normally whip-sharp brain of his.

Instead of backing off, he glared in return. "Maybe I can't win with you, but I know I can't win without you. I need you. Those are the facts."

As the pressure of his fingers diminished, the pain and anger dimmed, and something new began to creep inside. Hope.

She stared at him, working to keep her eyes hard and firm. Somebody needed to be smart in this relationship. "What are we going to do, Sam?"

"It's not that big of a deal."

"But Martin said…"

"I fired him. You'll meet my new manager tomorrow. Part of the agreement was that you're part of the campaign. I can't change my heart, Mercedes. I can't create love by the polling numbers. I don't want to be that kind of candidate. You don't want me to be that kind of man because that's not who you fell in love with."

"Sam…" she pleaded, knowing that she was weakening. It was the voice, that one-in-a-million voice, that slayed her. And the name on his lips was hers. Only hers.

"Come home with me, Mercedes. Max misses you. And there's a toothbrush with your name on it, and I miss your ziti." He stood there, saying the words that at one time she would have run from. They were permanent. As unchanging and as stubborn as he was. She wanted to believe him, she wanted to trust him, but there was a defenseless kid inside her, who knew with an absolute certainty that Santa Claus didn't exist, Cinderella had been a wuss, and that men would always run away. Mercedes couldn't understand why he didn't want to run away from her, too. "Why do you love me, Sam?"

"Because I can't *not* love you, Mercedes. It's just there, inside me, inside my heart. You're there."

"Sam…"

He put his arm around her, guiding her to 8th avenue. "Now don't talk, you'll only confuse yourself by arguing. I've got this all worked out. You keep your apartment in the city. We'll get you a driver's license with a Manhattan address on it."

"I don't drive."

He stopped. "You're kidding."

"No."

He shook his head, started walking again. "If you live in Jersey, you have to learn how to drive. But okay, we're getting off-track. You keep the New York address, so if anybody asks, you can tell them you're a New Yawker, why, I don't know, but—"

Mercedes stopped, smiled, and he looked at her. "What?"

"You're not going to leave me, are you? Ever."

"No. Heck, I wouldn't have made a spot for your toothbrush if it wasn't forever. What sort of idiot does that? I know you think I'm just a pretty face, but give me some credit for having some smarts, huh?"

She flung her arms around his neck, and planted a kiss on him. A long, wet, smoochy kiss. Taxis honked, people yelled, and Mercedes kissed him as if her life depended on it.

Finally, she lifted her mouth from his, and met his eyes. His green (not hazel) eyes looked a little drunk, a little bemused.

"What was that for?"

She grabbed his hand and started to walk. "Forever."

THE DAY OF ANDREW and Jamie's wedding was chilly and clear. The skies were cast-iron gray, the leaves were long gone, and the first hint of snow flirted in the air.

It was a perfect day.

The bride was beautiful in a Vera Wang dress that was classical, yet modern. The groom looked amazingly handsome in an old-style Oleg Cassini tux accessorized with a goofy grin, and everyone in attendance agreed the day was perfect.

For Mercedes, it was.

She cried during the ceremony, laughed when Jamie stuffed Andrew's mouth full of cake, and coughed nervously when Jamie blasted the bouquet right at her.

There were no white doves, the bride did not arrive in a horse-drawn carriage, although Andrew had still arranged to have orange blossoms scattered down the aisle, and Jamie didn't seem to mind.

Now it was almost time for the bride and groom to leave in their white Hummer limo, modified with all sorts of obscene suggestions appropriate for the occasion. It'd taken Mercedes and Jeff three hours to perfect the car, any opportunity to make Andrew blush was a chance well taken.

At the foyer in the hotel's reception hall, Mercedes picked up ten bags of rice, mainly to pelt her brother with, and smiled as Sam swung open the door.

Maybe there was another reason today was perfect. Maybe it wasn't just about Andrew and Jamie. This was about yesterday, and the yesterday before that, and the yesterday before that. Every day was the same. He was there, as reliable as the sunrise and sunset. Always there. And as the yesterdays started to stack up, fears for the tomorrows weren't quite so nerve-racking. She knew he was going to be there tomorrow, too.

At the sight of Sam on the steps, flashbulbs popped, reporters jockeying for position to get photos of the official Congressional challenger for New Jersey's Fifteenth District.

Mercedes moved back, out of habit, out of fear, but Sam smiled, tugged her hand, and pulled her forward.

"Not today, guys," he told the news crews, with his usual cheery grin. The cameras still followed, though, and the *Star-Ledger* ran a front-page picture of Sam Porter holding the hand of one Mercedes Brooks for all the world to see.

Epilogue

SAM'S CAMPAIGN KICKED into high gear. His television show was changed from a daily to a weekly, and he spent the next two months leaving the house before sunrise, and trudging home long after the sun had set. Mercedes stayed away from the cameras as much as possible, letting him steal the time that he needed.

Election night came, and Mercedes went with Tony and Sam to the ballroom at the Trenton hotel where the huge television monitors displayed the latest polling numbers. It was closer than Mercedes would have wanted, closer than it should have been, but in the end the people of New Jersey spoke and agreed with her. Sam Porter was their man.

When the other candidate conceded, reporters gathered around Sam, peppering him with questions, Mercedes discreetly stood back and watched, but there was a proud smile on her face. A big smile. How could she not love him? How could anyone not love him? He talked about politics at first, but then the personal questions started.

"Congressman, what about your affair with Miss Brooks? Do you think that affected your campaign?"

It was the moment she'd been dreading, this wasn't fair to Sam, and her stomach clenched.

Sam looked at Mercedes, then looked at the photographers. "I've always believed in being honest and calling things like they are. I know Mercedes affected the campaign, but not in the way you're expecting. A man needs to hear the opposing viewpoints, or he can't represent all of the people of this great state. A man needs to listen to opposing viewpoints, or he'll never learn. And sometimes, a man should agree with the opposing viewpoints, because it's the right thing to do. Mercedes keeps me honest, and gives me the hope I need to try and change things, try and make things work better. And one last point. Don't call this an affair. That implies something temporary and brief. This is neither temporary, nor brief. I'm in love with Mercedes and plan on marrying her as soon as humanly possible."

Instantly, the bright lights turned in her direction, blinding her momentarily. Here was the fame and recognition that Mercedes had always craved. But she didn't notice. Not now. She moved toward Sam, and smiled. He was all she craved, all she noticed.

He stared at her with green (not hazel) eyes, a question there.

"What about it, Miss Brooks? Is this true?"

She ignored the microphone and looked at Sam. "Yes. It's true. Today, tomorrow, forever."

* * * * *

Mediterranean Nights

Join the guests and crew of Alexandra's Dream,
*the newest luxury ship to set sail on the
romantic Mediterranean, as they experience
the glamorous world of cruising.*

*A new Harlequin continuity series
begins in June 2007 with
FROM RUSSIA, WITH LOVE
by Ingrid Weaver*

*Marina Artamova books a cabin on the luxurious
cruise ship* Alexandra's Dream, *when she finds
out that her orphaned nephew and his adoptive
father are aboard. She's determined to be reunited
with the boy...but the romantic ambience of the
ship and her undeniable attraction to a man
she considers her enemy are about to
interfere with her quest!*

Turn the page for a sneak preview!

Piraeus, Greece

"THERE SHE IS, Stefan. *Alexandra's Dream*." David Anderson squatted beside his new son and pointed at the dark blue hull that towered above the pier. The cruise ship was a majestic sight, twelve decks high and as long as a city block. A circle of silver and gold stars, the logo of the Liberty Cruise Line, gleamed from the swept-back smokestack. Like some legendary sea creature born for the water, the ship emanated power from every sleek curve—even at rest it held the promise of motion. "That's going to be our home for the next ten days."

The child beside him remained silent, his cheeks working in and out as he sucked furiously on his thumb. Hair so blond it appeared white ruffled against his forehead in the harbor breeze. The baby-sweet scent unique to the very young mingled with the tang of the sea.

"Ship," David said. "Uh, *parakhod*."

From beneath his bangs, Stefan looked at the *Alexandra's Dream*. Although he didn't release his thumb, the corners of his mouth tightened with the beginning of a smile.

David grinned. That was Stefan's first smile this af-

ternoon, one of only two since they had left the orphanage yesterday. It was probably because of the boat—ac-
cording to the orphanage staff, the boy loved boats,
which was the main reason David had decided to book
this cruise. Then again, there was a strong possibility the
smile could have been a reaction to David's attempt at
pocket-dictionary Russian. Whatever the cause, it was
a good start.

The liaison from the adoption agency had claimed
that Stefan had been taught some English, but David had
yet to see evidence of it. David continued to speak,
positive his son would understand his tone even if he
couldn't grasp the words. "This is her maiden voyage.
Her first trip, just like this is our first trip, and that
makes it special." He motioned toward the stage that had
been set up on the pier beneath the ship's bow. "That's
why everyone's celebrating."

The ship's official christening ceremony had been
held the day before and had been a closed affair, with
only the cruise-line executives and VIP guests invited,
but the stage hadn't yet been disassembled. Banners
bearing the blue and white of the Greek flag of the ship's
owner, as well as the Liberty circle of stars logo, draped
the edges of the platform. In the center, a group of musicians and a dance troupe dressed in traditional white
folk costumes performed for the benefit of the *Alexandra's Dream*'s first passengers. Their audience was in a
festive mood, snapping their fingers in time to the music
while the dancers twirled and wove through their steps.

David bobbed his head to the rhythm of the mando-
lins. They were playing a folk tune that seemed vaguely
familiar, possibly from a movie he'd seen. He hummed
a few notes. "Catchy melody, isn't it?"

Stefan turned his gaze on David. His eyes were a striking shade of blue, as cool and pale as a winter horizon and far too solemn for a child not yet five. Still, the smile that hovered at the corners of his mouth persisted. He moved his head with the music, mirroring David's motion.

David gave a silent cheer at the interaction. Hopefully, this cruise would provide countless opportunities for more. "Hey, good for you," he said. "Do you like the music?"

The child's eyes sparked. He withdrew his thumb with a pop. *"Moozika!"*

"Music. Right!" David held out his hand. "Come on, let's go closer so we can watch the dancers."

Stefan grasped David's hand quickly, as if he feared it would be withdrawn. In an instant his budding smile was replaced by a look close to panic.

Did he remember the car accident that had killed his parents? It would be a mercy if he didn't. As far as David knew, Stefan had never spoken of it to anyone. Whatever he had seen had made him run so far from the crash that the police hadn't found him until the next day. The event had traumatized him to the extent that he hadn't uttered a word until his fifth week at the orphanage. Even now he seldom talked.

David sat back on his heels and brushed the hair from Stefan's forehead. That solemn, too-old gaze locked with his, and for an instant, David felt as if he looked back in time at an image of himself thirty years ago.

He didn't need to speak the same language to understand exactly how this boy felt. He knew what it meant to be alone and powerless among strangers, trying to be brave and tough but wishing with every fiber of his being for a place to belong, to be safe, and most of all for someone to love him….

He knew in his heart he would be a good parent to Stefan. It was why he had never considered halting the adoption process after Ellie had left him. He hadn't balked when he'd learned of the recent claim by Stefan's spinster aunt, either; the absentee relative had shown up too late for her case to be considered. The adoption was meant to be. He and this child already shared a bond that went deeper than paperwork or legalities.

A seagull screeched overhead, making Stefan start and press closer to David.

"That's my boy," David murmured. He swallowed hard, struck by the simple truth of what he had just said.

That's my *boy*.

"I CAN'T BE PATIENT, RUDOLPH. I'm not going to stand by and watch my nephew get ripped from his country and his roots to live on the other side of the world."

Rudolph hissed out a slow breath. "Marina, I don't like the sound of that. What are you planning?"

"I'm going to talk some sense into this American kidnapper."

"No. Absolutely not. No offence, but diplomacy is not your strong suit."

"Diplomacy be damned. Their ship's due to sail at five o'clock."

"Then you wouldn't have an opportunity to speak with him even if his lawyer agreed to a meeting."

"I'll have ten days of opportunities, Rudolph, since I plan to be on board that ship."

* * * * *

*Follow Marina and David as they join forces
to uncover the reason behind little Stefan's
unusual silence, and the secret behind
the death of his parents....*

*Look for FROM RUSSIA, WITH LOVE
by Ingrid Weaver
in stores June 2007.*

HARLEQUIN®

Mediterranean NIGHTS™

Tycoon Elias Stamos is launching his newest luxury cruise ship from his home port in Greece. But someone from his past is eager to expose old secrets and to see the Stamos empire crumble.

Mediterranean Nights
launches in June 2007 with...

FROM RUSSIA, WITH LOVE
by *Ingrid Weaver*

Join the guests and crew of *Alexandra's Dream* as they are drawn into a world of glamour, romance and intrigue in this new 12-book series.

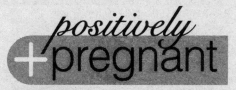

SILHOUETTE

SPECIAL EDITION™

COMING IN JUNE

HER LAST FIRST DATE

by *USA TODAY* bestsellling author

SUSAN MALLERY

After one too many bad dates, Crissy Phillips
finally swore off men. Recently widowed,
pediatrician Josh Daniels can't risk losing his
heart. With an intense attraction pulling them
together, will their fear keep them apart?
Or will one wild night change everything...?

positively +pregnant

**Sometimes the unexpected
is the best news of all....**

REQUEST YOUR FREE BOOKS!

2 FREE NOVELS PLUS 2 FREE GIFTS!

Red-hot reads!

HB07

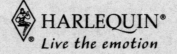

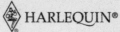

HARLEQUIN®

Blaze™

COMING NEXT MONTH

#327 RISKING IT ALL Stephanie Tyler
Going to the Xtreme: Bigger, Faster, Better is not only the title of Rita Calhoun's hot new documentary, but it's what happens when she falls for one of the film's subjects, undercover navy SEAL John Cashman—the bad boy who's very, very good....

#328 CALL ME WICKED Jamie Sobrato
Extreme
Being a witch isn't easy. Just ask Lauren Parish. She's on the run from witch-hunters with a hot guy she's forbidden to touch. Worse, she's had Carson McCullen and knows *exactly* how good he is. Maybe it's time to be completely wicked and forget all the rules.

#329 SHADOW HAWK Jill Shalvis
ATF agent Abby Wells might be madly in lust with gorgeous fellow agent JT Hawk, but she's not about to do something stupid. Then again, walking into the middle of a job gone wrong—*and* getting herself kidnapped by Hawk—isn't the smartest thing she's ever done. Still, she's not about to make matters worse by sleeping with him. *Is she?*

#330 THE P.I. Cara Summers
Tall, Dark...and Dangerously Hot! Bk. 1
Writer-slash-sleuth Kit Angelis is living a *noir* novel: a gorgeous blonde walks into his office, covered in blood, carrying a wad of cash and a gun and has no idea who she is. She's also sexy as hell, which is making it hard for Kit to keep his mind on the mystery....

#331 NO RULES Shannon Hollis
Are the Laws of Seduction the latest fad for a guy to snag a sexy date, or a blueprint for murder? Policewoman Joanna MacPherson needs to find out. Posing as a lonely single, she and her partner, sexy Cooper Maxwell, play a dangerous game of cat and mouse that might uncover a lot more than they bargained for....

#332 ONE NIGHT STANDARDS Cathy Yardley
A flight gone awry and a road trip from hell turn into the night that never seems to end for Sophie Jones and Mark McMann. But the starry sky and combustible sexual heat between the two of them say they won't be complaining.... In fact, it may just be the trip of a lifetime!

www.eHarlequin.com

HBCNM0507